"If You Want Me To Quit Pursuing This, Then Tell Me Now."

She closed her eyes. "If I said I don't want to be with you, I'd be lying to both of us."

Aidan bent and rested his lips at her ear. "You don't know how tough it's been for me, giving you space when that's not what I want to give you at all."

"I've had enough space." And she had. Wise or not, she wanted to be with him.

He answered by lining her neck with kisses, while she hoped for a little action on her lips.

Corri vaguely recognized the danger in behaving so recklessly at the office, but she didn't care. She only cared about finally having what she'd longed for, and thought about frequently, for the past two days—another one of Aidan's deadly kisses.

Somehow she worked her way into his lap. "The door..."

Dear Reader,

I must confess that over the past few years I've developed an aversion to cooking. I attribute my disdain to pouring all my creativity into writing. And until they invent a computerized stove that allows me to prepare a meal with a few keyboard strokes, I don't see a reversal in my attitude. Knowing that, you can probably imagine my family's delight when my oldest daughter graduated from a culinary academy. At least now they can be assured of a good meal when she comes to visit, and I can be assured of gaining a few pounds.

I find it amazing that my child, the chef, can take what's on hand in my pantry and freezer—which usually consists of pasta and chicken—add some olive oil and spices and come up with a gourmet dish. She still insists that I'm a good cook and never criticizes my penchant for preparing simple food. However, she has criticized—gently, of course—my less-than-exemplary skills when it comes to chopping vegetables. "Hacking," I believe she calls it. And from that came the inspiration for the opening scene in *Executive Seduction*.

If you enjoy watching other people cook, you should appreciate what happens when things get too hot in the kitchen between a celebrity chef and her gorgeous producer…and love wasn't originally on the menu.

Happy reading and *bon appétit!*

Kristi

KRISTI GOLD

EXECUTIVE SEDUCTION

Published by Silhouette Books
America's Publisher of Contemporary Romance

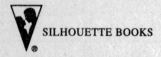

SILHOUETTE BOOKS

ISBN-13: 978-0-373-76768-7
ISBN-10:   0-373-76768-4

EXECUTIVE SEDUCTION

Visit Silhouette Books at www.eHarlequin.com

Printed in U.S.A.

KRISTI GOLD

admits to having a fondness for watching major league baseball, eating double cheese enchiladas and creating dark and somewhat dangerous—albeit honorable—heroes. She considers indulging in all three in the same day as the next best thing to a beach vacation!

Kristi resides in central Texas with her retired physician husband and the occasional guest in the form of one of her three grown children. She loves to hear from readers, and can be contacted through her Web site at www.kristigold.com or through snail mail at 6902 Woodway Drive, #166, Waco, TX 76712. Please include a SASE for response.

To my wonderful daughter, Lauren Ashley,
who wears the chef's hat in the family, and
who has brought me much joy over the years.

One

What a cowardly way to say goodbye.

In total disbelief, Corinna Harris stared at the Dear Jane letter resting on the pink marble vanity in her dressing room, a nice little missive that had been couriered to her only minutes ago. She shouldn't be surprised that her erstwhile fiancé had chosen this method to break it off. After all, Kevin O'Brien was a journalist, well-versed with the written word, although this particular correspondence was simple, and to the point.

Thanks for everything, Corri, but it's time to end it. Feel free to keep the ring. It's been fun.

Fun? After an eight-month sham of an engagement, one would think he might actually have had enough courtesy to tell her in person that it was over. Not that she was at all surprised. Not that she wasn't angry.

Corri yanked the one-carat diamond off her finger and hurled it across the room like a missile, where it hit the wall and landed somewhere in the thick blue carpet. If it happened to get sucked up in a vacuum by the cleaning staff, then too bad. She wanted absolutely no souvenirs of a relationship that had basically been a lie.

The rap at the door jolted Corri back into the reality of what she had to do—her job. "Five minutes," one of the crew called.

"Okay. I'm ready."

Was she really ready? Could she actually step in front of an audience and pretend nothing had happened? And today of all days, during her first live performance, a show centered on preparing the perfect holiday meal for lovers. Six days before Christmas.

Of course she could do this. Kevin might have temporarily screwed up her life, but she refused to let his careless disregard screw up her career.

After slipping on her favorite white chef's smock, the one covered with tiny wooden spoons, Corri did another quick check of her makeup and tightened her ponytail. A few tears threatened behind her carefully painted eyes, but she wouldn't allow them to fall. Instead, she got mad. Clung to the anger as tightly as a bank robber clutching his pilfered booty.

That alone sent her out to face the crowd, a fake smile carefully in place. She glanced toward the control booth and immediately spotted Aidan O'Brien, AOB Productions' owner, and Kevin's older brother. Since the day she'd taped her first show, Aidan had always been there, serving as her champion and friend. And at a good six foot three, he wasn't easy to miss. But it wasn't only his imposing height that earned attention. He had his Armenian mother's thick brown hair and olive complexion, his Irish father's incredible green eyes, and an air of concrete confidence that made some men cower—as well as an undeniable sense of mystery that made women long to know his secrets.

Speaking of secrets, Corri briefly wondered if Aidan had known about Kevin's plan. Of course not. He would have told her. At least she thought he would. He'd served as her confidante on more than one occasion, and they'd had more than their fair share of conversations, even if she'd done most the talking. Even if she hadn't been totally honest with him about her relationship with his brother.

Corri had the strongest urge to run to Aidan, cry on his broad shoulder and curse Kevin's bad timing. Not a banner idea. She had to weather this storm alone, and the first step entailed going out and giving her best to her fans.

"Thirty seconds," the stage manager called, and when he reached ten, counted down the seconds one by one, keeping time with Corri's erratic heart.

"Ladies and gentleman. Please welcome Houston's sweetheart of the stove, Corinna Harris, the star of *Hot Cooking with Corri!*"

Corri strode to the evergreen-bedecked stage on legs as stiff as wooden spoons, trying to take comfort from the rousing applause. But she felt only numbness, until, she considered that every time she'd walked onto this set for the past few months, she'd talked about Kevin.

Then the anger returned. She'd pretended that their relationship had been made in heaven, when, in fact, he'd given her a lot of hell.

And right then she decided that several ways to exact revenge did exist. Nothing like a woman scorned behind a stove.

The minute he saw her walk onstage, Aidan knew something was wrong with Corri. She was a tall, leggy, powerhouse blonde with as much appeal as the meals she served up to her audience, and for the past year, he'd scheduled his meetings around her popular weekly show. In that time he'd learned to gauge every move she made, every detail of her body language. Every detail of her body, period.

He probably should feel guilty that he spent a good deal of time studying Corri's finer points, particularly since she was engaged to his brother, but he didn't. No one knew he fantasized about her frequently. No one would ever know that he regretted introducing her to Kevin. But back then, he'd been in a relationship and by the time it had ended, Kevin and Corri had become a solid couple. So solid that they'd become engaged in a matter of weeks. For months he'd watched her talk about his brother during the show, and while her fan base had welcomed it, Aidan hadn't. In fact, at times he'd hated it.

Still, he firmly believed mixing business with pleasure could lead to problems in the workplace. But there had been days when he'd wondered about what might have been. Right now, he still wondered over

Corri's mood. She made it through the first three-quarters of the show without a hitch, but she'd sounded overly cheerful. Normally she cracked a few jokes, connected with the audience, but today she looked as if she only wanted to get it over with. Probably a solid case of nerves brought on by the live telecast.

Following the final commercial break, Corri resumed her show to conduct the usual question-and-answer session. But instead of calling on an audience member, she said, "We're going to do something a little different today in the time we have left."

She moved behind the island workstation and propped both palms on the edge. "Now that we've discussed a holiday meal guaranteed to jingle your partner's bells, we shouldn't forget those who don't have a lover during the season. Particularly the unfortunate few who have been jilted by some jerk at the worst possible time."

When Corri grabbed two hot pads, Aidan noticed the stage director standing offstage, flipping through the script and looking altogether confused. Corri pulled a pan from the oven, turned and slammed it down onto the butcher-block counter. "I suggest you go ahead and make this chocolate soufflé because you're going to want to eat the whole thing, and that's okay. But for the sake of your health, I also suggest you make a salad first."

After she tossed the hot pads aside, Corri turned to the refrigerator, and the production assistant muttered, "What in the hell is she doing?"

"Don't panic, Parker," Aidan said. "Corri's a professional. Let her go."

The control-room director didn't appear to care for

that answer. "We can't just let her go when we don't
know where she's going on live TV."

Aidan held up a hand to silence everyone when Corri
returned to the counter with an armload of vegetables
that she dropped onto the surface, seeming not to care
when a tomato rolled onto the floor.

She held up a large cucumber. "Let's start with this.
Just remember, it's not anatomically to scale, even if
most men would have you believe it is."

Parker shot a forlorn look at Aidan. "She didn't
just say that."

"Yeah, she did," the sound engineer said.

And something told Aidan she wasn't quite done.

Following a spattering of laughter, Corri slapped the
cucumber onto a cutting board, then picked up a nearby
cleaver. "When you're thinking about the idiot who's
left you high and dry, just imagine this is…" She looked
up and grinned, and that's when Aidan saw the hint of
tears. "Well, you catch my drift."

Then she began hacking away at the vegetable with
a vengeance, leaving the studio's occupants stunned
and the director demanding a fade-out.

But before the commercial could be cued, one young
woman called out, "What are you and Kevin doing for
the holidays, Corri?"

Corri looked up, cleaver still in hand, and sent the lady
a withering look. "I'm not doing anything with Kevin
over the holidays, because the jackass dumped me."

For someone who prided herself on composure, Corri
had just hit an all-time low on the no-self-control scale.

She didn't know what had gotten into her, why she'd perhaps let Kevin's little stunt ruin the best job she'd ever had. With several whacks of a cleaver, she'd shredded any possibility of a wider syndication beyond the region. And when the knock came at the dressing-room door, she expected to find a band of studio executives swooping down on her like a flock of hungry hawks.

She snatched a tissue from the holder and removed what she could of the mascara smudges beneath her eyes. "Come in."

"What's going on with you?"

Corri wasn't all that surprised to see the mirrored reflection of Aidan standing at the door. He was in charge of the studio, which meant he was in charge of her.

She spun around on the stool and shrugged. "I just made a total fool of myself."

He strolled into the room, hands in pockets, and stood there, silently studying her. "Go ahead, Aidan," she said. "Tell me I'm fired. Tell me you're going to cancel the show. Tell me a team of censors is waiting outside to wash my mouth out with soap. Just say *something*."

He took a couple of slow steps toward her and stopped, as if he feared she might go after him with the metal nail file set out on the vanity. "First, you tell me what Kevin did to you."

She slid the letter off the counter and offered it to him. "This came about ten minutes before the show."

Aidan took the paper and scanned it before muttering, "Son of a bitch."

Corri pulled the band out of her ponytail and began

to brush her hair with rapid strokes. "I knew this was inevitable. I just didn't think he'd handle it this way."

Aidan laid the letter down and leaned a hip against the vanity. "You two been having problems?"

She tossed the brush into a drawer, which she slammed a little harder than necessary. "Our entire relationship has been one big problem, Aidan. But I really don't want to talk about that now. I want to talk about the repercussions I'm going to suffer because of my behavior."

"We won't know for a few days," he said. "Whatever happens, I'll handle it."

She had no doubt he would, or at least try. "And that means determining what segment of my audience was most offended. The more conservative viewers, or the men."

"I'd say your male viewers. Every man in the control booth crossed their legs simultaneously when you went after that cucumber." He topped off the comment with a half smile.

She had to love him for trying to lighten the mood. "It was definitely not one of my finer moments, but I was so furious at Kevin I couldn't think straight. I'm sorry."

"If it makes you feel any better, I'm not happy with him, either." He folded the letter and slid it into his inside jacket pocket. "Do you know where he is right now?"

Corri knew where she'd like to send him—someplace without the benefit of air conditioning or any of those high-dollar hair products that Kevin so loved to use. "If my memory serves me correctly, he should be about to leave for the airport. He has a six o'clock flight to Baltimore to do a feature on some football player for the magazine."

Aidan checked his watch and pushed away from the vanity. "It's four o'clock, and Kevin's never on time. If I leave now, I might be able to catch him at the apartment. If not, I'll drive to the airport."

That plan didn't sound particularly wise to Corri. "What are you going to do, Aidan?"

"Have a talk with him."

She slid off the stool and realized how fragile she felt standing across from Aidan. She was five feet, nine inches tall, and not many men made her feel so delicate. "If you think you're going to somehow change his mind about breaking off the engagement, don't bother. It's been doomed from the beginning."

"I'm not going to try to talk him out of anything. As far as I'm concerned, you're better off without him."

Obviously the familial blood between them was running thin. "He *is* still your brother, Aidan."

"And his behavior impacted one of the studio's most valued commodities."

Corri appreciated his support, although she wasn't sure how she felt about being known as a commodity. Corri the Commodity. That fit. That was exactly what she'd been to Kevin. "If I can't talk you out of confronting him, then promise me you won't do anything stupid. I've done enough stupid things for both of us today."

"I'll be sure to make certain all sharp objects are out of my reach." He leaned over and swept a soft kiss across her cheek. "Now go home. I'll call you later."

After Aidan left the room, Corri touched her

fingertips to the place where his lips had been only moments before, totally taken aback by the gesture. Aidan had never been a cheek-kissing kind of guy. He wasn't prone to random bouts of affection. He wasn't the type of man who openly displayed any emotions unless it involved disapproval. Even then he used a hard, controlled tone and cutting looks as his weapon of choice, although he'd never really practiced those on her. He'd never had any reason to…until today. Yet he'd kissed her cheek instead.

And then she remembered that day last March. Remembered another kiss. For months now, she hadn't let herself think about it. But she thought it about it now.

It had all started with that silly, I'm Not Irish, But You Can Kiss Me Anyway T-shirt she'd worn to Lucine and Dermot O'Brien's house for their annual St. Patrick's Day party, right after she and Kevin had started going out. She'd received a few friendly pecks on the cheek from the O'Brien brothers—except for Aidan. She'd ended up with him in the kitchen—his mother's kitchen, no less—alone.

And then it had happened. *The kiss.* Unplanned, unexpected and anything but innocent. Corri had felt so guilty, she'd practically sprinted back into the living room to join Kevin, then she'd feigned a headache so he would take her home. The following weekend, she'd accompanied Kevin to Jamaica and returned engaged, for reasons unbeknownst to everyone. And later, she'd learned that Aidan and his long-time girlfriend had called it quits, for reasons she still didn't know.

One thing she did know. Overtly sexy men meant only one thing—trouble. Aidan O'Brien definitely fell into that category. And the last thing she needed was more trouble.

Fortunately for Aidan, Kevin's car was still parked in the garage at his condominium. Unfortunately for Kevin, Aidan was in no mood for socializing. He wasn't exactly sure what he would say to his brother, but he could guarantee it wouldn't be pleasant.

He rapped on the door three times before Kevin finally answered, looking disheveled and shirtless, as if he'd just crawled out of bed. Considering the clothes strewn all over the room at his back, he probably had.

Kevin ran a fast hand through his hair. "Hey, big brother, what are you—"

Aidan shoved him aside, walked into the living room and pulled out the letter. "What in the hell were you thinking?"

Kevin eyed the paper then collapsed onto the couch. "Corri sent you."

Aidan strode to the sofa and loomed over him. "Corri didn't want me to come. But I'm here now, and you have some explaining to do, so you damn sure better get to it."

After propping his bare feet on the coffee table, Kevin leaned back and stacked his hands behind his head. "I don't have a lot of time to get into this. My flight leaves in three hours, and I've already had to change it once due to another appointment. Besides, this isn't any of your damn business."

Aidan would wager that his brother's so-called appointment wasn't at all work-related. "I'm making it my business, Kevin. You could have been man enough at least to end it in person."

"I don't like messy goodbye scenes," Kevin said. "It's a lot easier to make a clean break without having to face someone."

That only angered Aidan more. "You're a coward, Kevin. You don't deserve Corri. You never have."

Kevin smiled, a smug one. "I guess you're going to tell me that you deserve her."

"I don't know what the hell you're talking about."

"Sure you do, Aidan. You've always wanted her, and for months now, you've been royally pissed off because I got there before you did. But now she's all yours, if you don't mind having my leftovers."

Aidan hung on to what was left of his composure, and tempered his tone when he said, "I'm not even going to justify that with a response."

Kevin came to his feet. "And I'm not going to ignore what Corri said about me on her show today. My boss's wife was watching, and she told him about it. I've just received a promotion to senior staff reporter at the magazine. If my position's in jeopardy because of Corri, I'm going to sue her and the studio for slander and defamation of character, I don't care if you do own the place."

Right when Aidan started to say that you couldn't defame a man with very little character, something caught his attention. Something that looked a lot like a cheerleading costume draped over the back of one dining-room chair. He crossed the room and picked up the sweater, noting it held the insignia of a professional basketball team. "Unless you're trying to get in touch with your feminine side, I'd say the owner of this is probably behind your bedroom door."

Kevin came at him quickly and grabbed the sweater away. "Get out, Aidan."

Aidan fisted his hands at his sides, resisting the urge to plant a left hook in his brother's jaw. They'd had the normal scuffles growing up, but not once had he slugged any of his brothers. Always a first time for everything. Then he considered something more effective. Something that could hurt Kevin worse, a direct blow to his professional reputation. "If you make any more noise about suing Corri, I'll have a talk with your boss myself. I'll let him know that you're more interested in screwing the pep squad than in doing your job."

Aidan didn't wait for Kevin's response before he was out the door, opting to nix the elevator and take the four flights of stairs in order to blow off steam. He hoped his threats worked, otherwise Corri could be in for a legal battle with her fiancé. Ex-fiancé, Aidan amended. That was the only good thing that had come out of this day.

Corri was no longer with Kevin, and that meant she was free to do as she pleased, and he would have no problem helping her get over his brother. He could make the fantasies a reality, even if it meant taking it slowly. Otherwise, she could run away again before he had his chance.

Two

For three hours, Corri wandered aimlessly around her apartment, picking up the clutter she'd ignored for several weeks. She'd never been a domestic goddess, although her kitchen was always spotless. Her bedroom was another story altogether. Her clothes tended to stay where they'd landed until she'd gathered them up to do laundry. Several pairs of shoes could be found lying in various places, some beneath her bed. She'd grown up in such a sterile environment, with everything always in its place, that she enjoyed the freedom of making a mess whenever she wanted, until she couldn't stand it any longer. And right now she couldn't stand it. She needed some order in her life. She felt as if she'd been strapped into a roller coaster, with no way to get off the chaotic ride.

Fortunately for her, on the few occasions Kevin had

visited her apartment, he'd never left any real reminders. For all intents and purposes, it was as if he'd never been there at all. Or even been in her life to any degree. Probably because he really hadn't.

When the doorbell buzzed, Corri worried it might be Kevin coming by to make amends at Aidan's insistence. If it did happen to be him, she would gladly take the opportunity to toss him out on his butt, as she should have done months ago. Yet, when she peered through the peephole, she didn't see Kevin. She saw his brother standing on her porch, and that was quite a surprise. Aidan had never paid her a visit before.

Corri opened the door, immediately regretting her unkempt state. "What are you doing here?"

He held up a brown paper bag. "I brought some wine. I thought you could use a drink."

She could. Several, in fact. "By all means, come in."

Aidan followed her into the living room and shed his jacket. "Nice place. Kind of a long drive from downtown."

"I like the quiet neighborhood." She liked the way he looked right now with his navy sweatshirt, well-worn jeans and loafers. Not that she'd seen him ever look anything but great. "You know, I'm so used to you in a suit, it's almost always a shock to see you in casual clothes."

"I guess we're even then," he said as he tossed his jacket over the back of one chair. "I've rarely seen you without all the stage makeup, or your hair down."

Her hand immediately went to her stringy hair. She hadn't bothered to dry it when she'd left the shower. In fact, she didn't remember brushing it. Not to mention, her T-shirt and sweats would qualify as too ratty to exist. "I'm a mess."

"You look great."

Considering the appreciation in his tone, she might actually start to believe it. "Thanks. Now come have a seat. I was just about to make something for dinner. Have you eaten yet?"

"No." He dropped down on the sofa and set the bottle on the table. "But you shouldn't have to cook. We could have Chinese delivered. Or pizza."

"Believe me, it's nothing fancy," Corri said on her way to the miniscule kitchen. Not unless he considered hot dogs fancy, because that's exactly what she'd planned to have. Nuked hot dogs. She'd gone to the grocer's on the way home and stocked up on junk food—major junk food, including double fudge cookies, and Italian soda. Tomorrow she could go to the gym and attempt to reverse the damage.

Corri microwaved three hot dogs, one for her and two for Aidan, and after gathering all the fixings and silverware, placed them on her nice teakwood tray. She opened the cabinet and took out the gold-rimmed wineglasses Kevin had brought her from Pamplona back in July, an attempt to make amends for missing her twenty-ninth birthday. If they weren't so pretty and ornate, she would happily throw one against the wall just as she had the ring.

After slipping a corkscrew in her pocket, and tucking the bag of chips under her chin, she carried the tray into the living room and slid it onto the coffee table. "Here you go. Franks à la Corri."

Aidan eyed the hot dogs for a few minutes. "The cloth napkins add a nice touch."

And they looked somewhat odd alongside the paper plates, Corri decided. But she was more concerned about pleasing Aidan. "I could whip you up an omelet if this won't work."

He grabbed the bottle of relish. "This is fine. I haven't had a hot dog since last summer at the ballpark."

Good, because Corri truly didn't want to go near the stove. She sat beside him, keeping a comfortable berth between them, yet still feeling oddly nervous. Ridiculous. He was her boss, her friend. But this was Aidan in her home, not in the office. "If you want some grated cheese, I could get that for you."

"This is fine." He picked up a knife and offered it to her. "Maybe you'd like to use this to vent some more frustration on your hot dog."

If he hadn't said it with such a sexy smile, she might have been insulted. "Very funny. I believe I've done enough hacking for one day." She handed him the corkscrew. "You can do the honors."

Aidan uncorked the wine with all the proficiency of a man who'd had a lot of practice. She had no doubt he'd done this on more than one occasion with more than one woman. Since his breakup with his former girlfriend, he'd dated quite a few eager prospects. Several had shown up at the studio like prime-time groupies asking for him, only to be turned away by Aidan's bulldog assistant, Stella. But as far as Corri knew, he hadn't been seriously involved with anyone lately. Not that that should matter to her.

He poured the merlot, then handed her a glass. "To good ratings."

Corri touched her glass to his. "I'll drink to that."
Right now, she'd probably drink to anything.

By the time Corri had eaten her hot dog, Aidan had
consumed both of his. She tore open the bag of chips
and tilted it toward him. "In case you're still hungry."

He waved them away. "No thanks."

Corri grabbed a few chips and set the bag down on
the table. "I shouldn't be eating them, either, but after
today, I'm in the mood to binge." She proved that by
consuming the chips in record time.

Aidan settled his gaze on her lips, then said, "Lean
over here."

She felt an abrupt surge of excitement. "Why?"

"Because you have mustard on your mouth."

Of course she did. What went better with bad hair and
no makeup than a blob of mustard? "Point it out, and
I'll get it."

"I'll do it."

She expected him to pick up a napkin. Instead, he
formed his palm to her jaw and rubbed the corner of her
lip with his thumb several times. "It's gone now."

If it was gone, then why didn't he move his hand
away? Why did he keep looking at her as if he wanted
a repeat of the kitchen kiss? And why was she wishing
he would kiss her? Easy. She wasn't in her right mind.

Finally, he let go of her face and took a long drink of
the wine. Corri settled back against the sofa, wine in
hand, and tried to think of something to say to break the
uncomfortable silence. She settled on a question she
should have asked the minute he came into the house.
"Did you find Kevin?"

His slight weight shift indicated a chink in his normal composure. "Yeah. At his condo. He hadn't left for the airport yet."

Apparently she was going to have to wring the information out of him. "What did he say?"

"He told me to mind my own business, and I told him he was a coward."

That gave Corri a strong sense of satisfaction. "You didn't punch him, did you?"

"No, but I wanted to when he mentioned suing you and the studio because of the show."

She pinched the bridge of her nose and closed her eyes. "I'm so sorry, Aidan. Normally he never watches the show."

"He didn't. His boss's wife did."

"Lovely."

"I made a few threats of my own, so you don't have to worry about it."

That called for a drink of wine, which she took before asking, "What kind of threats?"

"I told him I'd tell his boss that his new senior staff reporter was engaged in activities not job-related when he was supposed to be in Baltimore."

"Then he did get the promotion."

"He didn't tell you?"

"No, he didn't." But that explained the breakup; he didn't need her anymore. "And he was with another woman." Something that came as no surprise to Corri.

"Yeah. Some cheerleader. And I'm sorry to be the one who had to break the news to you." Although he didn't sound at all sorry.

Corri kicked off her flip-flops and curled her legs beneath her. "I'm not shocked, Aidan. As I've said, mine and Kevin's relationship had disaster written all over it from the beginning."

He studied her straight on. "I don't understand. If you knew it wasn't going to work, they why in the hell did you agree to marry him?"

She really hadn't planned to tell Aidan—or anyone for that matter—the reasons behind her engagement. Frankly, she was embarrassed over the whole thing. But since he'd played white knight for her this afternoon, he deserved an explanation. And if that destroyed their friendship, then she probably deserved it, considering her stupidity. "It's a long story."

"I've got all night, so let's hear it."

Corri drew in a deep draft of air, finished her wine and set the empty glass on the tray. "The trip to Jamaica back in March involved a conference with several of the magazine's executives, including Kevin's boss. Kevin explained that Ed and his wife were very conservative, so he convinced me it would be better if we said we were engaged."

Aidan held up his hands. "Wait a minute. The engagement was a farce?"

It sounded so sordid to Corri, most likely because it was. "You could say that."

"Then why didn't you set everyone straight when you came home?"

This was where it became complicated. "Kevin wanted to keep up the pretense until he secured his promotion, and that took much longer than he predicted. I attended all the parties with him as his fiancée because he believed it would look better if it appeared he was settling down."

Aidan leaned forward and raked a hand down his face. "You're a smart woman, Corri. I can't believe you went along with it for nine months."

"I planned to end it much earlier, but after Freed got wind of the engagement and decided to incorporate the whole impending marriage scenario into the show, and then my ratings soared, I couldn't do it. Instead, I chose to keep up the act."

"Freed's only producing your show because I handed it to him. You should have come to me."

"And I still might have lost my dream job. You and I both know the ratings were shaky before I left on the Jamaica trip."

He fell silent, and when Corri couldn't take it any longer, she said, "I know you think I'm insane. And believe me, I've questioned my sanity over the past few months."

"That whole scene today. Was that an act?"

She stared at her hands now folded in her lap, too ashamed to look at him. "No, it wasn't. I was really hurt by what Kevin did. The anger was real."

"Then you did care about him."

She had, at least in the beginning. "I wouldn't have done what I did for someone I hated. Although I have to admit, there were times when he did things to me…" She drew in a deep breath and blew it out on a sigh. "Never mind. It's no longer an issue."

A flash of anger crossed Aidan's face. "Tell me what he did to you."

"It's not what you think." In reality, he hadn't done anything to her, or with her, in a sexual sense. A fact she wasn't ready to disclose. "When we originally agreed to the engagement, we also agreed to continue dating. Kevin interpreted that as dating not only me, but several other women throughout the country. I finally decided I wasn't ever going to be enough for him."

"Kevin's never been in a steady relationship with anyone for any length of time," Aidan said. "He's not going to change, and that's no reflection on you."

Corri had definitely learned that the hard way. "You know, I've always been a confident person, comfortable in my own skin. But Kevin made me doubt myself, and that's what I've hated most."

"You're a beautiful woman, Corri, even if my brother was too blind to see it."

"He can be very charming."

"He's spoiled," Aidan said. "When we were growing up, he got away with murder while the rest of us had to toe the line. That's my mother's fault. Kevin was the sickly twin, and they almost lost him when he was born, so she's always gone out of her way to defend him, no matter what he's done."

"Oh, my gosh. Your mother." Corri covered her face with her hands. "She always watches the show. She must think I'm horrible."

Aidan draped an arm over the back of the sofa and lightly touched her shoulder to gain her attention. "You don't have to worry about that. My parents are in Wisconsin, visiting with my dad's sister. They won't be back until Christmas Eve."

Corri felt some measure of relief, although having to face the O'Briens was inevitable. At least she had a few days to prepare. After Christmas, she would drop by and have a talk with them. "I hope no one will tell her before I have the chance to explain everything."

"I doubt any of the siblings are going to make her the wiser. And I'm fairly sure Kevin isn't going to be the one to drop that bomb, at least for a while."

Mental exhaustion began to set in, bringing about Corri's yawn. "I'm just too tired to think about anything right now."

Aidan patted her thigh and stood. "Then I'll let you go to bed."

When he offered his hand to help her up, Corri took it without hesitation and came to her feet. "I wouldn't blame you if you decide not to be my friend any longer."

"You don't have to worry about our friendship, Corri. And even if I'm still having trouble getting a handle on what you've told me, on some level I understand it."

"You do?"

"Yeah. We're both obsessed with our careers, and we're willing to go to great lengths to succeed."

Considering Aidan was only thirty-five, he'd accomplished quite a bit. And that prompted several questions in Corri's mine. "What lengths have you gone to?"

"It's another long story. I'll save it for some other time. Now walk me to the door before you drop where you stand."

When they made it to the entry, Corri gave him a hug before pulling back. "Thanks so much for listening."

Surprisingly, Aidan kept his arms around her. "Now I'm going to tell you something I've never told you before."

Corri wasn't certain she could take anymore shocking news. She wasn't sure she could think with Aidan so close. "This sounds serious."

"It is." Placing his palm on her lower back, he nudged her a little closer. "You know that red apron you wear every now and then on the set?"

"Sure. It's one of my favorites."

"Mine, too. I've imagined you wearing it…and nothing else."

Okay, this could be too much for her to handle. "I don't know what to say, Aidan."

"You don't have to say anything. But if you want someone to take your mind off your problems, I'm here. Whatever you need, you only have to ask me, and I'm not talking about only work-related needs."

She needed him to quit staring at her with those captivating green eyes. She needed to quit looking at that to-die-for cleft in his chin, and above that, those incredible lips. She had personal knowledge of how incredible they were, and exactly how they would feel if he kissed her. She wished he would, even if that wasn't the greatest idea.

He moved her hair back from her shoulder, but instead of pressing his lips against her lips, he brushed a warm, lingering kiss on her neck, right below her ear. "Remember, if you need anything, Corri, all you have to do is ask."

Before she could even recover from that simple,

albeit sexy gesture, before she could answer his proposition, he was out the door. And she must be out of her mind to be so incredibly attracted to Aidan after what she'd been through. One O'Brien brother in her life had been quite enough, even though Aidan was the polar opposite of Kevin.

He was also extraordinarily sexy. And strong. And tempting. Tonight she had noticed the little things about him, like how his green eyes seemed to change color at times—darker when he was serious. Lighter when he smiled, which he didn't do often enough. Of course, if he did, she would be melting like a good chocolate fondue on a regular basis.

Corri shook herself out of the daze and forced herself back into reality. Through her parents' example, she'd learned to avoid overriding chemistry in a relationship at all costs. Once the passion between Bridgette and James Harris had played out, there had been nothing left—except an adolescent girl who'd become caught in the middle of her parents' ongoing war for years.

For that reason, among others, exploring more than friendship with Aidan was very ill-advised, because if the underlying passion finally exploded, she wasn't certain she could resist being in Aidan's line of fire.

When the head-turning man entered the crowded exercise arena, Corri did a double take, and almost hurled herself off the treadmill before she had the presence of mind to turn the thing off. For a split second, she'd thought she was about to confront her past.

She should have known it was Kieran, not Kevin, coming toward her, even though they were mirror twins. Over the months, she'd come to recognize the physical differences. They shared the same dark hair and eyes, but Kieran was left-handed, and much more buff. That stood to reason considering he was a personal trainer and owner of three successful gyms, including the one she was standing in at the moment.

When Kieran reached her, Corri smiled, even if an exact replica of her ex-fiancé was the last thing she wanted to see right now. "Hey, Kieran."

"Hey, Corri." He straddled the weight bench next to the treadmill. "I'm probably the last person you want to see right now after Kevin's stunt."

She added *mind-reader* to the list of differences. "Then you've heard all about it."

"I saw it," he said. "I made sure the show was on in the gyms yesterday afternoon."

Oh, great. The physically fit population of Houston was probably questioning her mental fitness. "Normally, I might thank you for that, but after my little tantrum, you might want to ban me in order to keep your male customers safe."

He grinned. "I'm not worried about that. I am worried about you, and I apologize for Kevin being an ass."

"It's not your fault, Kieran. I know you're not your brother's keeper."

"Don't think I haven't been in the past, Corri. He's done some pretty unforgivable things to me. So if you want me to beat him up, let me know. I've been looking for another good excuse for a while now."

At least most of the O'Brien brothers had honor, even if Kevin hadn't retained that from the gene pool. "Aidan's already had a talk with Kevin. Not that it did any good."

"I'm surprised Aidan didn't lay him out, considering how he feels about you."

"He's a good friend," she said.

Kieran gave her an incredulous look. "You think that's all he wants to be to you, Corri?"

"I have no reason to believe anything else." Not exactly the truth. Though she'd consciously denied the subtle signs for months, they had always existed: in the heated looks he gave her, in the light touches that to most people would appear innocent. In the way he said her name—and somehow she knew exactly how it would sound coming from his mouth if he made love to her—soft, low and sexy. And she couldn't discount last night, or that day in the kitchen....

"What about that kiss back on St. Patrick's Day?" Kieran asked, hurling Corri out of her mental musings.

My gosh, he *was* psychic. Her mouth dropped open momentarily before she snapped it shut. "You know about that?"

"Almost everyone knows about it."

Great. Just great. "Define *almost*."

"If you're worried Mom knows, don't be. But all the boys, including Kevin, know about it. I'm not sure about Mallory or Dad."

And she thought she'd suffered all the shock humanly possible in the past two days. "Did Aidan tell you?"

"Are you kidding? Aidan never tells anyone anything. Kevin saw the two of you together."

Corri found the fact that Kevin had never mentioned it unfathomable. "Does Aidan know everyone knows?"

"I doubt it. It's no one's business but yours and Aidan's."

She flipped a hand in dismissal. "It doesn't matter anyway. It was just one of those things. Something that happened months ago. I'd forgotten all about it."

Kieran looked doubtful, and rightfully so, considering Corri was lying. "Whatever you say. But I tell you one thing, if given the chance, Aidan would be with you in a heartbeat. And a word of warning. When Aidan wants something, he always gets it, so be prepared."

Aidan hadn't been prepared for Corri storming into his office, wearing a pair of black form-fitting yoga pants and a bright-blue windbreaker. Her hair was piled on top of her head, with a few gold strands framing her flushed face. Every inch of her shouted sex, and Aidan's libido was definitely listening.

After closing the door, she leaned back against it as if her legs might not hold her up. "I'm glad you're here."

He could say the same thing to her. "I thought I told you to stay home for a few days."

"I went to the gym and ran into Kieran. He told me something I wanted to share with you."

When she strode to his desk at a fast clip and braced her hands on the edge, he recognized she meant business. "Did you know Kieran knows about the kitchen?" she asked.

He closed the lid on his laptop and kept his gaze

trained on her face, even though he wanted to give her a slow once-over. "I take it he saw the show yesterday."

"Not *that* kitchen." She pulled back the chair opposite him and collapsed into it. "I'm talking about that day at your parents' house back in March. At the party. In your mother's kitchen. In fact, he told me all your brothers know about it, including Kevin."

That would probably explain Kevin's persistence in pursuing Corri. His little brother was nothing if not competitive. "I really don't give a damn who knows about it, Corri. I didn't take you up against my mother's china cabinet." Aidan tried to push away the images that comment evoked, without success. "It was only a kiss."

"I know what it was," she said. "I was there, remember?"

"Yeah, you were there, and I've never forgotten one moment of it. In fact, I remember every detail."

"I remember it was a huge mistake."

Someday soon, he planned to remind her how good it had been. Right now, he needed to focus on business, not on a memory that he'd relived on more than one occasion. "Have you checked your e-mail today?"

She looked surprised by the sudden change in topic. "I decided to wait a while to do that."

"I've already taken a look."

Her hand went to the zipper on the jacket, lowering it and raising it compulsively, giving Aidan a glimpse of her breasts encased in tight white knit. "How bad is it?"

If she didn't halt the peep show, it could get bad. In two minutes, he was going to round the desk and take off her damn jacket, and he might not stop there. "Most of the e-mails were from women, and supportive. A few were from men, offering to console you. One guy sent a one-word message."

"What was that?"

"'Ouch.' And some jerk specifically asked you to dinner, as long as you let him pat you down before you got in his Lotus."

Finally, she smiled. "A Lotus, huh? That might be worth a pat-down."

It would be a frigid August in Texas before Aidan allowed that to happen. "Now you have to decide if you want to go ahead with the pre-New Year's Eve taping next Wednesday, or let me pre-empt with one of your other shows."

She mulled that over a minute before saying, "I'll do the taping. It will give me the chance to apologize to the fans."

Aidan reached behind him and grabbed the next item of business that he definitely didn't like. "Speaking of New Year's Eve, you're still scheduled to participate in the children's charity fund-raising auction."

She rubbed her forehead. "I'd totally forgotten about that. Are you sure they still want to auction me off?"

"According to Stella, they called this morning to confirm it. But you can back out." He hoped she would. He didn't like the thought of some guy paying for a date with her.

She stared off into space for a minute before saying, "It's for a good cause, so I'll do it. Besides, it's only dinner afterward. What's the worst that could happen?"

She might encounter someone who wanted to take

her mind off her troubles before he had that opportunity. But he still had time, and patience. "I'll let Stella know. That's it for now."

"One more thing." She leaned forward and folded her hands on the desk in a death grip. "Did you record the show on your TV?"

"I did this time because it's a live airing." He recorded her show every time so he could analyze her…in non-business-related ways. "Why?"

"Because I didn't. I was so nervous, I forgot. If it's okay, I thought I might watch it at your place this afternoon. I could do that here, but I'd rather witness my downfall in private."

He wasn't certain she was emotionally ready to see the tape, especially not alone. "Are you sure you don't want to give it a couple of days?"

"No. I'd rather get it over with. I'm hoping it's not as bad as I think it is. If you'll let me have your key, I'll have it back to you before you leave this evening."

Aidan refused to leave her at his house by herself. He depressed the intercom and when Stella answered, said, "Tell Freed something's come up and I need to reschedule our meeting for after lunch instead of during." Without waiting for his assistant's response, he turned his attention back to Corri. "I'll go with you."

"That's not necessary, Aidan. Unless you're afraid I might pilfer all the valuables before I leave, or leave a trail of mangled vegetables in my wake."

He stood and came around the desk. "I'm not worried about any of that. Since you've never been to my house, you don't know where it is."

"Now that you put it that way…" She pulled a set of keys out of her pocket. "I'll drive us."

Aidan wasn't going to argue that point. He'd let her call the shots for now, until he found the right time, and the right way, to convince her to give up some control.

Three

Chagrined, Corri handed over the remote control to Aidan and lowered her head. "I've definitely seen enough." And she had, right down to the maniacal look in her eyes when she went after the cucumber.

"Are you sure? I can play it back in slow motion, so we can get the full effect of the cleaver action."

She had a good mind to push him off his perch on the arm of his expensive beige suede sofa, right onto his gorgeous butt. "I'm glad you think this is funny, because I don't. I looked like a raving lunatic."

"You looked moderately pissed off."

Moderately was definitely an understatement. "I can't stand the thought of your mom and dad watching this."

Aidan pointed the remote, selected Erase and wiped out the recording with the push of the button. "Now you don't have to worry about them seeing it here. And since they don't own all the latest technology, I doubt they have it recorded."

Corri hated deceiving people as wonderful as Dermot and Lucine O'Brien. But then she'd been lying to them about Kevin, and that brought about more shame. "I dread seeing them again, and that's if they even *want* to see me again." Just one more thing Kevin had taken away from her.

"You're practically one of the family, Corri," he said. "My mother considers you her second daughter."

And that in itself presented a huge problem. "*Was* one of the family, Aidan. But not now."

Feeling restless, Corri came off the sofa and strolled around the large den, stopping at the floor-to-ceiling window to take in the impressive view. The house was situated in a gated community several miles from downtown. She'd definitely been surprised by the location, and the surroundings in general, including a pristine lake and several fountains. The interior design was patently masculine, with contemporary decor that suited Aidan.

"Anything in particular you want to do now, Corri?"

Startled, she spun around and almost lost her balance, saved only by the fast grab of Aidan's lapels. He gave her that look again, the one he'd brought out last night when she'd thought he might actually kiss her. The one he'd given her on St. Patrick's Day.

Since the window was at her back, she had nowhere to run, even if that's what she wanted to. Funny, she didn't feel like moving at all. But she needed to move—

away from him instead of toward him, otherwise she might be making another foolish mistake. "You could give me the grand tour of the house. Unless you need to get back to the studio."

"Freed can wait." He braced his palm above her head. "I'm in no hurry to get back."

Neither was Corri, although she probably should be. But considering she'd have to return to an empty house and no doubt obsess over the show, spending a little more time with Aidan would provide a welcome diversion. "Lead the way."

"Follow me."

Corri trailed behind Aidan through the formal dining area and into a huge kitchen straight from her dreams of what a kitchen should be. The appliances were stainless steel, top of the line, right down to the double oven and state-of-the-art refrigerator. She ran her hand over the black granite countertops and muttered, "Incredible."

"I take it you approve."

She turned and leaned back against the counter, discovering Aidan had put the center island between them, probably a good thing. He looked so appetizing, she could very well forget herself in the kitchen again. "It's amazing. Have you ever used it?"

"Only the microwave. But you're more than welcome to use it anytime. In fact, maybe we should initiate it soon."

He rounded the island and walked toward her, all cool, deliberate confidence dressed in a blue designer suit and sporting a heated gleam in his green eyes. This time, Corri could easily move aside, get out of his path.

But again, she didn't care to do that, not even when he planted his palms on either side of the counter and leaned into her. "It's definitely not my mother's kitchen, but it will have to do."

And after months of shutting out the memories, Corri waited anxiously for a repeat of that March day, knowing she shouldn't. And when Aidan finally kissed her, she realized she hadn't forgotten one detail, either, although the reality was much, much better than the recollection.

Aidan O'Brien had taken the art of kissing to all-time heights. He started out slowly, softly, almost a tease before he slid his tongue inside her mouth. The heady sensations brought about those inevitable chills, that predictable heat, the sense that she would gladly remain this way for hours. In his arms. Under his spell.

Without warning, he lifted her up onto the cabinet, taking his place between her parted legs. With one hand, he lowered the zipper on her jacket, slowly, slowly, then formed his palms to her sides, his thumbs lightly stroking her ribcage.

Had Corri been able to claim any reticence to that point, it would have disintegrated the minute Aidan palmed her breasts, stroked her nipples through the knit, made her want to know how his hands would feel on her bare skin.

But as quickly as he'd broken down all her resistance, he broke the kiss and dropped his hands to her hips. She saw the desire in his eyes, heard it in his voice when he said, "I could have my fly down in two seconds and make love to you right here, right now." He lifted her jacket's zipper back into proper position. "But…"

But? But what? This was no time for buts, not when

Corri was so willing to let him have his wicked way with her before her common sense came back around.

He lowered his head and angled his body away. "I have an appointment in less than an hour to discuss your show."

Corri felt as if she'd been dowsed by a bucket of ice water. Okay, slightly cool water. The heat still hadn't quite dissipated, even if her job had horned in on the moment. "Shouldn't I be there at the meeting?"

Aidan held out his hand and helped her down from the counter. "Let me take care of this, Corri."

He reeled her back into his arms and slid one hand over her hip before subtly brushing his fingertips across her belly. "And someday soon, I plan to take care of your other needs, too."

"I suppose it could be worse, Aidan."

Freed Allen's monotone was starting to grate on Aidan's nerves. "Corri's going to survive this. In fact, she'll probably come out of it more popular than before."

"You could definitely say that," Parker Hampton added. "I got a call from a friend at the cable network. It's rumored they're going to make Corri an offer after the first of the year."

Nothing Aidan didn't already know. Her agent had said as much to him at a cocktail party the week before, even if a firm deal wasn't in place, and Corri hadn't been apprised of the possibility. As much as he despised the thought of her leaving the studio, that opportunity rarely came along in the business, and it would be wrong to keep Corri from realizing her potential.

"Did the cable channel see her last show?" Freed asked.

"Yeah, and from what I understand, they don't care," Parker said. "But that's the cable mantra. If it's controversial, then go for it."

Aidan's self-interest kept intruding, in spite of his attempts to halt it. "It's not a done deal, so let's move on."

"But if it does go through, that means we would have to let her out of her contract," Freed said. "We'll have to take a look at that."

Aidan's mood was quickly deteriorating. "We're not going to do anything yet. And what's been said in this room goes no further until we have confirmation."

Parker raised his hands, palms first. "I'm not going to say a word."

"Nor will I," Freed added.

Aidan tossed his pen aside and leaned back in his chair. "Unless anyone has anything else to add, this meeting's over."

Freed stood first. "I only have one more thing to say. We're letting Corinna slide this time, but if she pulls another stunt like the last one, then she's gone."

Aidan gave him a hard look. "That's my decision to make, not yours." Unfortunately, he couldn't guarantee Corri wouldn't have another episode like the last, particularly if someone did something to anger her. Which meant he needed to proceed with caution.

"I'm counting on you to see she behaves herself from now on." Freed spun around like a member of the color guard and marched out of the room.

Parker hadn't moved an inch, and that only made Aidan more irritable. "What is it, Hampton?"

"Just a quick question. Is something going on between you and Corri?"

He wanted to tell the production assistant it wasn't any of his damn business, but that would only fuel Parker's speculation. The last thing Corri needed was to become the brunt of studio gossip. "She was engaged to my brother. Beyond that, we're friends."

"Friends. Right." He came to his feet. "Then let me make a suggestion. Stop looking at her like she's Sunday brunch and you haven't eaten all week."

With that, Parker was out the door, not giving Aidan an opportunity for denial. He picked up the pen, chucked it at the wall and watched it make a perfect landing in the potted plant. He'd always been good at hiding his personal affairs, even when he'd worked closely with Tamara and they were sleeping together, before everyone knew they were a couple. He didn't understand why he was having such a tough time keeping his attraction to Corri under cover. Why everyone seemed bent on butting into his business.

From this point forward, he'd make sure no one knew that he wanted Corri, even if it meant avoiding her until things calmed down.

Corri wasn't sure what she had done to warrant Aidan's avoidance for the past two days, but she planned to get to the bottom of it, and soon.

Fifteen minutes ago, she'd told Stella to ask Aidan to meet her in the dressing room, the place she always retreated to plan her upcoming menus. For the past five minutes, she'd been staring aimlessly at the laptop,

regretting she'd agreed to go forward with the New
Year's show. Normally she wouldn't dare consider
something as traditional as a ham, but simple might
work better than trying to cook a duck without making
a mess of it. Or cooking her own goose again.

When she heard the door open, Corri kept her attention focused on the half-baked menu. She didn't want
to seem too anxious, even though she wanted to spin on
the stool and demand answers.

"What do you need, Corri?"

She glanced at the mirror to see him standing behind
her before focusing on the screen again. "I'm trying to
decide whether to go with vichyssoise or a spicy green
chili corn chowder. Cold versus hot, kind of like the
mood around here lately."

He moved closer and propped his palms on the back
of the vanity stool. "Are you angry about something?"

She snapped the laptop closed. "Of course not. Why
should I be angry when I have no idea whether I have a
job because the boss hasn't spoken to me in two days?"

He swiveled the stool around. "If you're wondering
why I haven't called you, I have my reasons."

"Care to share for a change?"

"First, I didn't have much to report on the meeting
other than that things are looking fairly good as far as
audience reaction is concerned. Second, I wanted to
give you some time to think about what's happening
between us."

She managed to wrest the stool back around so she
could think without having to look at his incredible
face, but unfortunately the mirror offered her a prime

view. "I'm not sure there's anything to think about, Aidan. I'm coming off a really bad relationship, and you're offering to help me get over it. I'm not sure I need to even consider that right now."

When he braced his hands on her shoulders, Corri's mind shouted, *Don't touch me or it will be all over.* Her body said differently, gifting her with a slow-burn heat surging through her.

Aidan made eye contact in the mirror. "I don't want to pressure you, which is exactly why I wanted to give you some time. If you want me to quit pursuing this, then tell me now."

She closed her eyes and tried to dredge up the stop-word, without success. "If I said I don't want to be with you, I'd be lying to both of us."

He bent and rested his lips at her ear. "You don't know how tough it's been for me, giving you space when that's not what I want to give you at all."

"I've had enough space." And she had. Wise or not, she wanted him.

He answered by streaming his palms down the front of her blouse, lingering for a moment at her breasts before traveling back to her shoulders again. He lined her neck with kisses, while she hoped for a little action on her lips. This time she whirled the stool around, and he immediately took the cue, pulling her up from her perch and straight into his arms. She vaguely recognized the danger in behaving so recklessly at the office, but she didn't care. She only cared about finally having what she'd longed for, and thought about frequently, for the past two days—another one of Aidan's deadly kisses.

Somehow they reversed roles and Aidan ended up seated on the stool. Somehow she'd worked her way into his lap, straddling his thighs. And somehow she managed to return to coherency long enough to say, "The door."

"It's locked."

For a moment she thought he'd planned this little bout of insanity, but then she remembered the door automatically locked and required a code for admission. For her protection, of course, although she wondered if she might need a little protection now to keep her from doing something totally brainless. But that thought drifted away when Aidan slipped the buttons on her blouse, and she loosened his tie and went after his buttons between more seriously steamy kisses. He formed his hands to her breasts through her silk bra, and she ran her hands up and down his chest.

So this was it, that overriding passion that made sensible women engage in foreplay in precarious places. This was that spontaneous combustion thing that made a level-headed girl from New Mexico forget herself, lose her mind. The very thing her own mother had warned her about. But she was on board the Aidan train, quickly bound for oblivion, and she didn't want to get off before the next stop.

When he released the button on her slacks, she met his gaze and saw the heat in his eyes—and wondered if she was getting too close to the fire. But what better way to crash and burn?

Someone rapped on the door, followed by Julie calling, "Freed needs to see you, Corri."

Corri cleared the haze from her brain before clearing her throat. "I'll be there in a minute."

Aidan dropped his hands to her hips. His chest rose and fell with broken breaths, his eyes closed momentarily as if he needed to ground himself before he pinned her in place with those gorgeous green eyes. "We can't do this here and risk someone finding out about us."

No kidding. "This is crazy, Aidan."

"This is chemistry, Corri. We can try to fight it, but this sort of thing will keep happening until you finally accept it and give in."

She knew exactly what it was. She just didn't know how to handle it. Moving off his lap would be the first step. She had to get away from him so she could think.

After climbing off the stool, Corri crossed the room, putting much-needed space between them before facing him again. "This is wrong."

He slid off the stool and strode to her, basically backing her up against the wall. "It's right, Corri. Or it will be as soon as I make it right. But doing what we're doing here, in the studio, isn't going to work."

"You didn't seem to mind where we were a few minutes ago."

"That's because I lose all reason around you." He cupped her jaw in his palm and kissed her lightly. "Come to my house tonight. I'll pick you up."

"I suppose I could make good use of your kitchen."

"That sounds like a good plan. I could think of several ways we could use the kitchen."

She rolled her eyes. "I meant I could make you dinner. Something special."

Of course, this little rendezvous had nothing to do with preparing a meal. He knew it, and so did she.

"I'll be at your place at eight," he said.

"That's too late." And she sounded much too enthusiastic.

"Fine. Seven then. I'll cut out of here early."

"I can drive myself." In case she decided to put an end to this foolishness and make a quick getaway. "I'll go by the store and pick up a few things. Would you like anything in particular?"

Right on time came the arrival of his lethal grin. "Yeah. Bring that red apron."

Corri couldn't believe she'd actually brought the apron. Worse, she was wearing it. Fully clothed beneath it, of course. She had a blue-cheese stuffed tenderloin and seasoned potatoes roasting in the oven, and asparagus ready to steam on the stove. Her internal burner was still set on high following the afternoon's make-out session, not that her temperature seemed to be of much concern to her host.

Since she'd arrived an hour ago, Corri hadn't seen that much of Aidan. He'd poured them each of glass of cabernet, and since then he'd been on the phone nonstop while she'd gone about preparing the meal. He had kissed her briefly on the cheek, and had made a downright dirty reference to the apron before he'd disappeared. She definitely didn't intend to serve the meal wearing only a scrap of red cotton just to cater to his whims, although that would be one surefire way to get his attention.

When Aidan walked into the kitchen, he came up behind her and circled his arms around her waist.

"Smells good," he said, then nuzzled his face against her neck. "You smell good. You look good, too."

She turned on the water and began shoving the vegetable cuttings down the drain. "Sure, Aidan. This apron really complements my drawstring pants."

He slipped his hand beneath the apron and landed it on her belly. "Drawstring, huh?"

Corri should have known better than to dangle a drawstring in front of a man. She flipped on the switch, setting the disposal into action. "Down, O'Brien."

He toyed with the string. "How far down do you want me to go?"

Corri had never seen this side of him before, but she suspected many women had, only one more reason for his astounding popularity with the ladies. Normally he was a man of few words. When he did talk, people listened. She was listening, or at least her body was. But she felt the need to put on the brakes for the time being.

She shut off the disposal and made the fatal mistake of facing him. She'd seen his face almost every day for a year, had looked into those green eyes on numerous occasions, but she was starting see him in a totally different light. And that could be dangerous. "Look, I'm still wondering if this change in our relationship is such a good idea."

He smoothed a fingertip over her jaw. "What are you afraid of, Corri?"

Him. Not exactly him, but how he made her feel. "I'm afraid we'll ruin our friendship."

He dropped his arms to his sides, his expression hinting at frustration. "I'm not going to apologize for wanting you."

She didn't want an apology. She only wanted her normally good instincts to tell her what to do. Yet she could only hear the sound of warning bells going off in her head. "We'll talk about it after dinner." That would buy her more time, and she definitely needed more time.

He backed up a few steps. "Fine, Corri. You're in charge from this point forward. I'll be in the den if you need anything."

Oh, she needed something all right. She needed to quit analyzing ad nauseum. Her desire for Aidan was primal, fueled by her own sexual urges. It didn't have to make sense. She didn't have to try to dig up some rhyme or reason for it. Their relationship didn't have to go beyond two people enjoying each other intimately. Nothing had to come of it. Nothing probably ever would. Eventually he would move on to the next conquest, and she would concentrate on her career goals.

That sounded so logical, which was why she couldn't quite explain that little ache, right around the area of her heart.

For the most part, she'd been silent during dinner. He'd tossed out a few compliments about the meal, and she'd thanked him. But he could tell that her mind was on overdrive, weighing all the pros and cons of taking this thing between them to the limit.

Aidan wanted to take it beyond the limit. He wanted to prove to her that she was a desirable woman. He wanted to undo all the damage his brother had done by leading her to believe otherwise. He wanted to know if the reality lived up to the fantasy, even though he inherently knew it would. He also didn't want to alienate her completely, the reason why he'd decided to let her call the shots. If she did decide she didn't want to move on to the next step, then he'd have to accept it. He wouldn't like it, but he'd deal with it.

When Corri stood and took their plates, Aidan followed her into the kitchen. "I'll do that later," he said. Right now he wanted to have a talk with her, even though that wasn't his normal game plan when he had a beautiful woman in his house. But nothing about this situation was normal.

She rinsed the first plate then put it in the dishwasher. "I don't mind cleaning up." When she reached for the other plate, he caught her wrist. "Come with me into the den."

She sent him a forlorn look over her shoulder. "What do you plan to do there?"

"Only talk, Corri." At least for the time being.

She dried her hands on a paper towel, then took off the apron and laid it on the counter before facing him. "Okay. Let's talk."

Once they'd settled in side-by-side on the sofa, Aidan opted to start with something he'd been meaning to ask her all evening. "What are you planning for Christmas?"

She toed out of her sneakers and crossed her legs before her. "I don't have any plans. My mother's going to be in Bermuda with her new boyfriend. My dad's going to be at his house in Delaware with the new wife."

"And you're not going to join either one of them?"

She shrugged. "If I spend the holiday with one, then I'll never hear the end of it from the other. From the time they divorced when I was a teenager, I've been a pawn in their ongoing battle. Frankly, I'm sick of it."

Aidan could understand that. He also couldn't tolerate the thought of her spending the day alone. "You can come with me to my parents' house."

Her dark eyes widened. "I can't do that. I really don't want to face Kevin—"

"He's not going to be there. Kieran told me he's taking a trip to Aspen."

"Of course he is," Corri said. "He promised me that trip back in May."

Aidan surmised his sorry brother had promised her several things, and hadn't followed through on any of them. "Since he's not going to be at the house, then I don't see any reason why you shouldn't be there."

"Don't be obtuse, Aidan. I'm not a part of your family any longer. No Kevin, no O'Brien family dinners."

"You can come as my guest. My parents expect you to be there."

"That's because they don't know about the end of the engagement. As soon as they find out, I'm sure they'll change their tune. In fact, I should tell them when they get back on Sunday since Kevin obviously isn't going to do it."

"I'll talk to them about it," Aidan said.

She shook her head. "I can't let you do my dirty work for me."

"Kevin's dirty work," he corrected. "I'm going to be

in charge of telling your side of the story before Kevin hands out his version. You can talk to them about it on Christmas Day."

She frowned. "Do you have this need to handle all my problems?"

He laid his palm on her thigh, right above her knee. "I'll handle anything you want me to handle." So much for his vow to slow down. But he'd be damned if she didn't look too tempting to ignore, with that tight gray long-sleeved knit shirt and those damnable drawstring pants. First things first. He leaned over and kissed her softly, then again, until she wrapped her hand around his neck and brought him in for the kill. And she was definitely killing him with every thrust of her tongue against his. Corri had taken control, and Aidan was losing his.

When he slid his hand beneath her top and traced the curve of her breast with his fingertip, Corri pulled back and groaned. "You're making it so hard for me to remember why we shouldn't be doing this."

"You're just making me hard, Corri."

He saw a brief flash of indecision in her brown eyes that quickly turned provocative. "Prove it."

He had no problem with that. As he had earlier at the studio, he lifted her onto his lap and positioned her legs to straddle his thighs, giving her the full effect of his erection. "Proof enough?"

She smiled, a shaky one. "Why don't we go to your bedroom and you can give me a little more proof."

"Are you sure about this, Corri?" A definite first for him. In the past, if a woman requested a trip to the bedroom, he didn't leave the topic open for debate.

When she climbed off his lap and stood, Aidan worried that she'd reconsidered. When she pulled her top over her head and tossed it on the table behind her, he realized he'd assumed wrong. And when she tugged that drawstring slowly, then shimmied out of her pants, he almost bolted from the sofa. Through sheer will alone, he waited to see what she might do next.

"Are you convinced now?" she said, her voice low but steady.

He took a minute to study her, raking his gaze down her body, now covered only in a sheer white lace bra and matching panties. He paused at the small silver ring in her navel, surprised since she didn't seem like the type of woman who went for body piercing. Not that he was complaining. It was sexy as hell. *She* was sexy as hell, from her long, long legs to the curve of her thighs and hips. The reality beat the fantasy by a mile.

She gave him a self-conscious look. "Are you going to continue to stare at me all night, or are you going to touch as well as look?"

That was all it took for him to join her. She clasped the hem of his sweatshirt and worked it over his head, then dropped it next to her shirt on the table. He pulled her flush against him, sent his hands in motion down her back and over her butt, taking the time to explore before they got down to business.

As he started backing her toward the hallway, the phone rang. When he backed her against the wall and kissed her, the machine clicked in.

And when Parker's voice announced, "The studio's

wet, Aidan. You need to get down here," Corri pulled back and frowned. "What did he just say?"

"Something about the studio being wet." He formed his palm between her thighs. "So are you."

"Obviously the studio is flooding. Doesn't that bother you?" She looked incredulous, but she sounded breathless.

Aidan recognized that a flooded studio should bother him. And yet he had another pressing issue straining against his fly. He braced his palms on the wall, and lowered his head. "I'm afraid if I let you go, you're going to start thinking again. And reconsidering."

"You have to see what's happening, Aidan. I need to see. What if the kitchen's ruined?"

Apparently she saw that as a good excuse to postpone the trip to the bedroom. As bad as he hated to admit it, she happened to be right. The studio was his livelihood, and it needed his immediate attention, even if she did, too.

Corri ducked under his arm and when Aidan turned around, he found her grabbing up her clothes. "I'm really sorry we didn't have the opportunity to finish this," she said.

Not as sorry as he was. He went back into the living room, snatched his shirt from the table and dropped back down on the sofa. "We are going to finish this Corri. Sooner or later. Unless you're going to tell me you've changed your mind."

She tugged her pants back into place and cinched the drawstring tight. "The phone call changed my mind. Otherwise, I was more than willing, in case you didn't notice."

"The scream was a dead giveaway."

"I did not scream."

He grinned. "Maybe not, but you wanted to. You were going to before the night was over."

She slapped him up the side of the head with her shirt. "You are so asking for it."

He caught her hand and brought her back onto the sofa beside him. "And I'm going to get it, Corri. I always get what I want." At least that's what he planned in this case. But plans sometimes went straight to hell in that legendary handbasket.

He kissed her again until she wrested away from his arms and stood, leaving him alone with an erection that showed no sign of disappearing in the immediate future. "You need to get dressed, Aidan."

He needed to get a grip, because right now, with her standing above him without a shirt, her hair a total mess, he was on the verge of telling Parker to handle the problems at the studio. He'd rather keep her occupied all night in his bed. Maybe even for the next few days. Maybe even the next few years....

Whoa, O'Brien. He wasn't sure where the hell that thought had come from. And right now, he didn't have time to investigate. He wasn't even sure he should.

Four

As she stood in a good two inches of water, Corri was beginning to believe that somewhere in the cosmos, a depraved wizard was trying to tell her to stay away from Aidan—and quite possibly warning her not to do the next show. Her life of late had been all about bad timing, and bad decisions. Which is why she needed to weigh this thing with Aidan before she made another mistake. But she had to admit he was a mistake she wouldn't mind making.

"It could be worse, Corri."

She glanced to her right to see Parker standing next to her, his red hair sticking up like cactus needles all over his scalp, as if he'd just left his bed. He probably had. She wished she had recently crawled out of bed. Aidan's bed. "How did this happen?"

"There was some kind of a minor leak under the sink. The plumber was here today and apparently turned it into a major leak."

"Apparently." Corri surveyed the area: water was covering the tiled floor and had seeped into the carpeted area in the gallery that housed the audience.

Aidan had stopped only long enough to check it out, then he'd disappeared. She hadn't seen him since. And because they'd driven in together, she didn't have any way to leave unless she called a cab.

"By the way, I have something that belongs to you." Parker fished through his pocket and pulled out *the* ring. "The nighttime janitorial staff found this in your dressing room and turned it in."

Great. The diamond had avoided the vacuum and found its way into the hands of an honest soul.

Corri took the ring and pocketed it. She'd decide at a later date how to dispose of it, although donating it to charity seemed like a fine idea. She wondered if a non-profit organization for victims of jerks existed. "Where's the boss?"

Parker hooked a thumb over his shoulder. "He's on the phone calling the restoration company to get them out here to start the clean-up."

"That's going to cost a pretty penny, bringing in a crew on a Saturday, and two days before Christmas, no less."

"Even if he didn't have insurance, which he does, Aidan can afford it."

His house alone indicated he was thriving financially, although Corri had no idea exactly how much money he made. The studio produced several successful shows, some that had gone on to national syndication, and others, like hers, that were more or less bartered to regional affiliates. Regardless, even if he was strapped for cash, he couldn't very well let the water sit and possibly grow mold over the holidays.

"I think I'll go find out if he's making any progress," she said before backing up a couple of steps.

"Were you and Aidan having a late-night meeting?"

Corri didn't like Parker's smug grin or the question. "We had a late dinner to discuss the upcoming show."

He took a quick check of his watch. "It's almost midnight. That's a really late dinner. Bad for digestion. As a chef, you should know that."

Without responding, Corri turned around and headed down the mazelike hall toward Aidan's office. Halfway there, a hand reached out and snagged her arm, pulling her into the break room, startling her so much that she had a hard time reclaiming her voice. "You nearly scared me to death, Aidan O'Brien."

He had the nerve to slide his hands down her back and over her bottom. "My apologies. I thought you might like some coffee since we're going to be here a while."

"Explain 'a while.'"

"Maybe an hour or two. The clean-up crew should be well into the process by then."

Corri hid a yawn behind her hand. "Maybe I should find a sofa and take a nap."

"Maybe I should join you on that sofa, but I don't want to sleep."

She laid her palms on his chest, intending to push

him away, and failing. He felt too good against her, too welcome and warm and sexy. "You better behave, Mr. O'Brien. Your production assistant is already questioning why we're together so late at night. I think he believes we're having a torrid affair."

He tucked a random strand of hair behind her ear. "I called his cell and told him to go home. That means we're alone until the crew arrives. We can do whatever we'd like, wherever we'd like to do it."

As tempting as that sounded, Corri still had a few concerns. "Do you know for certain that Parker's already gone?"

"No."

"Then do you think it's wise for us to engage in questionable activities at the risk of being discovered?"

He mulled that over for a minute before releasing her. "You're right. It's too risky."

"If you're free tomorrow evening…" Corri glanced at the clock on the wall, noting midnight had come and gone. "I guess I should say if you're free tonight, I'd be glad to cook for you again. Or we could actually go to dinner somewhere."

"I have a noon flight tomorrow to New York. I'm not coming back until Sunday."

Must be that wizard again dictating her destiny. "Maybe some other time then."

"You're coming with me."

"Excuse me?"

"You heard me. First-class flight. Five-star hotel. Dinner with people I know in the business. Good contacts."

As tempting as his offer might be, Corri had a lot to

consider. "By the time we finally get out of here, it's going to be very late. I'd have to pack."

He brought his arms back around her and tugged her closer. "You only need a dress for dinner, and something to wear on the return trip. You don't need any clothes for bedtime."

Corri thought she might shiver right out of her shoes. "I still need to finish planning the menu for the show."

"You'll have most of the day Sunday and all day Tuesday."

"You skipped Monday."

"You're going to be with me on Monday, at my parents' for Christmas lunch."

"So we're back to that again?"

"Right now, I'm not going to argue with you. I am going to kiss you, though."

And he did, right on the lips, not holding anything back, until Corri felt as if she could dissolve and seep into the carpet like the flood waters on the set. Once they parted, he looked at her expectantly and said, "Well?"

"Is that, well, am I going to join you on Christmas day, or well, am I going to go with you to New York?"

"Let's start with New York."

"Are you absolutely sure you want me there?"

"If I didn't, I wouldn't have asked. We can be together without any interruptions."

Corri mulled that over for a minute, and a strong sense of déjà vu hit her full force. A weekend getaway, with an O'Brien brother, dinner with colleagues and another possible pretense. "Will we be staying in the same room?"

He looked at her as if she'd taken leave of her senses. "Of course."

"You're not worried what your friends might think?"

Awareness dawned in his expression. "I'm not Kevin, Corri. What we do in the privacy of a hotel room is our business. And I'm sure as hell not going to ask you to pretend we're engaged."

"Then you'll introduce me as your friend?"

"Yeah." He smiled, slowly. "With perks."

That definitely said it all. Friends with benefits, a term that had quickly become a cliché. Of course, she didn't want anything else from him. She didn't expect any ever-after or long-term commitment. Only a nice diversion in the hands of a man who had seduction down to a science. She could definitely live with that for the time being. "Okay, I'll go."

He kissed her again, quicker this time, but the impact on Corri was still as strong. "You won't regret it, Corri."

She hoped she wouldn't, but something told her she might.

He had a well-appointed suite with a king-size bed at his disposal, and a naked woman in the bathroom. And there he was, alone on the sofa in the living area, staring out the window, unable to appreciate the view of the New York City skyline. He had half a mind to call Farino, bow out of the dinner and join Corri in the made-for-two shower. But he'd already agreed to this meeting, so he might as well see it through. He could wait a few hours until he had Corri alone tonight, and since she'd slept most of the plane ride, she should be well-rested, even if he wasn't. Yeah, he could wait a few more hours.

Or maybe not, Aidan's next thought when Corri entered the room wearing a sleeveless, classy, curve-hugging red dress, a pair of matching spiked heels dangling from one hand.

She walked to the sofa and stared down at him. "Do you approve of my outfit?"

He inclined his head and took a lengthy visual inspection. Her sleek, straight golden hair trailed past her shoulders and framed the collar that circled her slender neck. The dress completely covered her cleavage, but the length showed a lot of her long legs. Aidan imagined in great detail taking off the dress, revealing little by little exactly what she had underneath it.

While he continued to survey the scene, Corri balanced on one leg and worked a shoe onto her foot. "You still haven't said if it's okay."

If it were any more okay, he'd make that call and cancel. "You look good." Too good. He didn't exactly embrace the prospect of taking her about town so every man they encountered could ogle her, including his friends.

She dropped down on the sofa beside him. "I wasn't sure if the red was a bit too much."

"Red's definitely your color."

When she leaned forward to slide the other heel on her foot, Aidan caught a span of bare back, starting from where her hair ended below her shoulders and plunging to her waist. "Where's the rest of the dress?"

She straightened and frowned. "I didn't realize it

was going to be so cold, otherwise I would have brought something with sleeves. But at least I did bring a coat."

Two more seconds and he was going to relieve her of her clothes, and his. Instead, he stood and faced her. "Are you ready?"

Corri came to her feet and moved right up against him. "You could definitely say I'm ready." She straightened his tie then leaned to nuzzle his neck. "You smell good."

"So do you." And when his hand automatically landed on her lower back, contacting smooth flesh, he realized she felt good, too.

"How long do we have to stay after dinner?" she asked.

As far as Aidan was concerned, they could leave immediately after the main course and have their dessert in bed. "Not that long. This isn't official business. Only required socializing between old friends."

For the first fifteen minutes in the upscale Manhattan restaurant, Corri had enjoyed visiting with two of Aidan's former network colleagues, the balding, forty-something Ben Farino and the wiry fiftyish Hal Shapiro. They were attentive, interesting and apologetic that the last guest had yet to arrive, although they hadn't identified said guest. Corri assumed she would soon be surrounded by four men, until she noticed the woman coming toward them. The kind of woman who prompted necks to crane everywhere she went. Her near-black hair, cut in a fringed bob complete with bangs, framed a face that displayed prominent cheekbones, full, coral-coated lips and almond-shaped turquoise eyes that nearly matched the color of her cut-down-to-there silk dress.

Men and women alike would consider her a truly classic beauty. Corri would have chosen another *B*-word to describe the mystery woman when she arrived at the table, said in a smoky voice, "Sorry I'm late, boys," then leaned over and planted a kiss on Aidan's mouth.

"It's wonderful to see you, Aidan," she practically purred, making Corri want to brandish her claws.

Aidan only nodded and muttered, "Tamara."

So this was the infamous Tamara Layton, the woman Kevin had told Corri about. Aidan's former lover who'd had his attention for almost four years. Corri tried to tamp down the sudden nip of jealousy, without success.

As soon as Tamara took her seat between Ben and Aidan, she laced her fingers together atop the table and leveled her gaze on Corri. "Who do we have here?"

A woman who doesn't like you. Corri offered her a fake smile, but not her hand since she wasn't feeling particularly gracious. "Corinna Harris. I'm a friend of Aidan's."

"Aidan has always been friendly with the women." Her tone reeked with sarcasm.

"Corri's the star of one of my shows," Aidan said. "She has quite a fan base."

Tamara arched a thin eyebrow. "You're an actress?" She sounded as if that occupation held sewer-level esteem.

Corri had every intention of setting her straight. "I'm a chef. I present a weekly show geared to meals for lovers."

Tamara sipped at her water. "How quaint."

"Tamara's the head writer for *Relentless Justice*," Hal said. "I produce the show."

"I haven't really watched it, but I hear it's a good series." That was the only nice thing Corri could come up with at the moment.

Tamara sent Aidan a blatantly suggestive look. "Aidan was my producer at the network. Before he decided to play cowboy and move to Texas."

Aidan gave her a champion scowl, which pleased Corri greatly. "It's Houston, Tamara. One of the five largest cities in the country. Not the wild, wild West."

Tamara rested her palm on Aidan's forearm with a familiarity that made Corri's blood simmer like boeuf bourguignon. "It's a whole world away from New York, Aidan. Surely you miss being here."

"Actually, I don't." Aidan cleared his throat and tugged at his tie. "We could probably use a bottle of wine now."

"I agree." Ben raised his hand to signal the waiter.

After that, Corri began to feel like a fifth wheel as the group talked about old times. Her only contribution came when Hal asked for dinner recommendations. By the time the main course arrived, Corri had no appetite left and, not long after, moved her barely eaten chateaubriand aside. She hated wasting a good meal, but she hated even more feeling as if she'd entered a galaxy whose inhabitants didn't welcome her. She also hated the way Tamara kept touching Aidan. Hated the way she kept tipping her head toward him to speak, as if she had the right. Corri realized she had had that right at one time, and that only made her more distressed.

Needing a few moments to regroup, Corri grabbed her evening bag, scooted back from the table and stood. "I'll be back in a few minutes."

She left without providing more explanation or sparing Aidan another glance. After finally locating the restroom, she entered the double doors, stepped inside an ornate lounge and sat on a plush mauve-and-gold striped chair situated in front of a white marble vanity. At least she felt somewhat more comfortable in a place that resembled her dressing room, with a little more flair, of course.

Corri rummaged through her purse, withdrew a tube of lipstick and applied a thin coat of razzle-dazzle red. As soon as she and Aidan returned to the hotel, he had some explaining to do. Of course, he wasn't obliged to tell her all the gory details of his relationship with Ms. Perfect, and she didn't particularly want to hear them. But he could have at least warned her that his ex-girl-friend was coming for dinner.

And coming into the lounge, Corri realized as Tamara breezed through the doors on a draft of exotic perfume. "I thought I might find you here," she said as she took the chair next to Corri's.

Grabbing a tissue from the built-in holder, Corri dabbed at her lips and checked her teeth for unsightly smears, and quite possibly fangs. "I needed to freshen my makeup." She needed to get away from the woman next to her.

When Tamara pulled a comb from her black silk purse and whisked it through her hair, Corri received some minimal satisfaction as static electricity created a few fly-away strands in Tamara's neat coif. Of course, Ms. Perfect withdrew a miniature hairspray and took care of it immediately.

"How long have you been Aidan's special project?" she said after dropping the bottle back into her bag.

Keeping her gaze centered on the mirror, Corri leaned forward and ran a fingertip below her bottom lid to remove non-existent mascara smudges. "I've been doing the show a little over a year now."

"I meant how long have you been doing Aidan?"

How long have you been such a busybody? "We're friends. I was engaged to Aidan's brother."

Tamara snapped her purse closed and sent Corri a wry smile. "*Was* engaged?"

Corri resisted the urge to chunk the crumpled tissue at Tamara's forehead and opted to discard it in the built-in trash bin. "For a few months. We've recently called it off."

"And Aidan rode in to pick up the pieces of your broken heart."

"My heart is quite intact," Corri said. "It was a mutual parting."

Tamara had the skeptic's expression down pat. "Well, considering the way Aidan looks at you, my guess is he'd prefer to be more than your friend, at least for the time being."

Taking about as much conjecture as she could endure, Corri scooted the chair back and stood. "I should probably get back now."

Tamara shifted to face her. "Before you go, some advice. Aidan's an extraordinary man in many ways, and he's an expert lover, if you don't already know that. The best I've ever had. But he's not very good at expressing his feelings, so you never know quite where you stand."

"As I've said, we're friends."

"He's grooming you," Tamara said.

"Grooming me?"

"Yes. And once you reach the pinnacle, he'll bow out of your life and move on to someone else he can mold into a success story. Or maybe I should say he'll make it easy for you to bow out of his life."

Corri refused to listen to another word from such a noticeably bitter woman. "I'm sorry things didn't work out between the two of you, Tamara. But my relationship with Aidan is different."

Tamara sent her a knowing and somewhat cynical smile. "You say that now, but another word of warning. Once you're caught in his web, you'll find it hard to escape. And if you make the mistake of falling for him, you're going to regret it before it's over. And eventually, it *will* be over."

Aidan trailed behind Corri as she rushed into the suite and tossed her coat and purse onto the end of the sofa. She'd been glued to the cab's door on the way to the hotel, acting as if he were radioactive. He knew why she was upset, but he wasn't sure what he could say to fix it. She'd been as blindsided by Tamara's appearance as he had. And as soon as he had a chance, he planned to call his friends and give them both a solid piece of his mind.

Right now, he needed to deal with Corri's distress. He refused to let the evening end on a sour note due to the unexpected appearance of a woman who meant nothing to him any longer.

Corri stormed into the bedroom while Aidan stopped

inside the door and leaned a shoulder against the frame. He decided to maintain some distance, at least until she calmed down.

She sat on the edge of the bed, slipped off her shoes and kicked them aside. "You could have given me some notice about your girlfriend," she said, the first significant words she'd spoken since they'd left the restaurant.

"Former girlfriend." He shrugged off his jacket and laid it across a nearby chair. "I had no idea she was going to show up. I was as surprised as you were."

After pushing off the bed, Corri walked to the bureau to remove her earrings, keeping her back to him. "You both seemed very happy to see each other. I got the distinct feeling she wanted to see a lot more of you."

He could only imagine Tamara's conversation with Corri, and he highly doubted it had been friendly.

Taking a chance, Aidan crossed the room and came up behind Corri. "What did she say to you exactly?"

She turned and leaned back against the dresser. "She didn't have to say anything. The fact that you knew each other very well was more than obvious. She kept touching you all through dinner, and you certainly didn't seem to mind."

Corri was jealous, and he had to admit that he liked her that way. He wanted her that way, even if she had no reason to envy Tamara.

Bracing both palms on either side of her, he leaned in closer. "Now we're even. For the past nine months, I've had to listen to you on the show, insinuating that you had a great sex life with my brother. And all that time, I had to deal with the fact that he was touching you." He brushed her hair away from her bare shoulder. "The way I wanted to touch you. The way I want to touch you now."

He noticed the fire in her brown eyes, the slight shiver as he ran his palm up and down her bare arm. "Then it's over between you and Tamara?" she asked in a tone that told him she remained unconvinced.

"It's all in the past, which is where I intend to keep it, regardless of what she might have told you."

She reached up, loosened his tied and slid it slowly from around his neck. "She did tell me you're an expert lover."

Now she was baiting him, and he was ready and willing to walk right into her trap. "Just say the word, and I'll let you be the judge."

She answered by wrapping one hand around his neck and pulling his mouth to hers. She kissed him without hesitation, without holding anything back. He vaguely thought he should take this to the bed, but the overriding heat between them didn't call for logic.

He lifted her onto the bureau, freed the hook at the back of her neck and lowered the dress's bodice. Only then did he break the kiss to take a good look, discovering she wasn't wearing a bra, exactly as he'd predicted. And she looked too good not to touch. But first things first.

Corri's chest rose and fell in rapid pants as he stepped back and tore at his buttons, losing a few along the way before he finally got the damn shirt off. Then he went back to her and rubbed his chest over her breasts, back and forth until she released an impatient sound.

When he lowered his head and drew one nipple into his mouth, she threaded her fingers through his hair, followed his movements, drove him insane when she took his hand and laid it on her thigh. He knew what she wanted, and no one could ever accuse him of not giving a lady what she wanted.

He slipped his hand immediately beneath her hem and stroked the inside of one thigh. "Unless you can give me one good reason not to, I'm taking you to bed."

Five

Corri could think of one good reason not to move: She might actually come to her senses.

"We don't need the bed," she said, and watched the surprise cross Aidan's face.

"You want it here." He posed it as acknowledgment, not as a question, right before he reached beneath her dress and slipped her panties away.

She expected him to do what he'd said he wanted to do a few days ago at his house—lower his fly and take her right there. Instead, he ran his knuckles along the inside of her thighs while fondling her breast with his free hand. Sheer torment, she thought as he made his way higher at an agonizingly slow pace. Sheer madness, she decided as she parted her legs wider, prompting Aidan to shove the dress up until it was nothing more than a fabric tube around her waist. Now she was completely exposed, vulnerable, and hotter than she'd ever been before in her life.

He lifted her arms around his neck and said in a deep, drugging voice, "I'm going to give you what you need."

She tipped her forehead against his chest and watched while he set his hand in motion between her thighs, stroking softly, inside and out. The scene was highly erotic, almost surreal, an experience to be savored before she could no longer think.

She also realized that Aidan wasn't at all unaffected, either, her theory supported by the rapid sound of his breathing, the perspiration where her arms met his shoulders. He was barely hanging on, as was she. He eased a finger inside her, continued to caress her, all the while telling her how good she felt, how hot she was, how he'd imagined this for months. For the past few days, when she was alone in bed, she'd allowed herself the fantasy, too.

But not like this. Never like this. Not once had she ever abandoned her power to such extremes with any other man. Not once had she felt so crazed with wanting. And never before had she experienced a climax with such force that she actually cried out.

Aidan kissed her hard and fast, then took a step back. She saw something almost feral in him—he was a man who prided himself on remaining cool and collected, even in extremely tense situations. He withdrew a condom from his pocket, and with his free hand, undid his fly, shoved down his pants and briefs. He tore open the package with his teeth, then slipped the condom on with hands that appeared to be shaking slightly, another sign of his faltering control, and that only excited Corri more. So did knowing that in a matter of moments, he was going to put an end to the ache, and return the passion to her life. No matter how dangerous that might be, she welcomed it. Welcomed him, or at least she would.

Clasping her hips, Aidan pulled her to the edge of the bureau while she clung to his shoulders. "Wrap your legs around my waist," he commanded. After she complied, he drove into her with one hard thrust, then another, stealing her breath and fueling her need.

He tempered the pace for a time, rested his lips at her ear and whispered, "You feel so damn good."

So did he, but she couldn't seem to find her voice to tell him when he drove into her, again and again. She was mildly aware of the sound of the mirror behind her hitting the wall, and was very cognizant that she was making love with an incredibly sexy man atop a marble-covered bureau in a high-class hotel room. Taboo in many ways, at least for her, and frankly she didn't care. She only cared about watching Aidan in action, the determination on his gorgeous face, the play of taut muscle beneath her hands, the feel of him deep inside her.

He kept his green eyes leveled on hers and his hands working wonders on her body, looking very much in command. Then she witnessed how his control began to slip, felt it in the tightening of his frame, heard it in the oath that spilled out of his mouth when she gave in to another orgasm. He thrust one more time, shuddered and stilled, then leaned heavily against her. She felt his weight sag slightly, and briefly wondered if he might buckle. Instead, he lifted her up and with his pants still wrapped around his ankles, shuffled to the bed and brought them both down onto the mattress in a heap.

Corri couldn't stifle her laughter. "For a second there, I thought you were going to drop me."

"I thought you were going to kill me. You're lucky I remembered the condom."

She would be lucky if she ever recovered. "I honestly don't know what got into me."

He pressed his hips against her. "In case you haven't noticed, I did."

Oh yeah, she'd noticed. "I meant I'm not normally that unrestrained."

He kissed the tip of her nose. "I appreciate your lack of restraint, even if I did plan for it to last longer. Those plans went straight to hell, thanks to you."

She smoothed her hands over his incredible butt. "Are you complaining, O'Brien?"

"Not in the least." Much to Corri's disappointment, he moved off her and said, "I'll be back in a minute, and I want you completely naked and in this bed waiting for me when I get back."

Corri couldn't think of anywhere else she'd rather be at the moment. "As long as you come back completely naked."

"You bet." He worked his way to the edge of the mattress, stepped out of his slacks and tossed them aside. Corri watched him cross the room, taking in the sight of his bare back and bottom, and thinking all the while she could not believe this had happened between them after all these months of only friendship. Worse, she couldn't imagine it not happening again. And again.

Aidan came out of the bathroom to find Corri covered up to her chin. When he reached the bed, he tossed two more condoms on the nightstand, grabbed the covers and yanked them back.

Corri immediately crossed one arm over her breasts and splayed her palm below her navel. "What are you doing?" She looked and sounded shocked. She also looked damn beautiful, from the top of her blond head to the bottom of her slender feet, and all points in between.

"I'm making sure you followed my orders," he said, taking a little more time to assess her body before he joined her again. "Move your arm and your hand away. I want to look at you."

Aidan noted a slight hesitation in her expression before she finally dropped her arms to her sides, stiff as a concrete barrier. "Relax, Corri. I've already seen you naked. I just want to take a closer look."

And he did, a long one. Her pale nipples hardened when he centered his gaze on her breasts. And when he visually tracked a path down to the light shading between her thighs, she shifted slightly. She was either feeling self-conscious, or she was hot again. He'd bet his stock portfolio on the latter. He planned to take care of that soon, but first he felt the need to talk to her about a few things, and that was a new concept for him. He wasn't one to go for after-sex dialogue. Now, when it involved business, he could converse with the best. But when it came to emotional issues, he was out of the zone. Tamara had reminded him of that time and again. Why he felt the need to be more open with Corri, he couldn't say, but he didn't plan to analyze that until much later.

Aidan stretched out on the bed and slipped his arm beneath Corri, bringing her against his chest. Formulating a conversation that would put her mind at ease about his ex would be a good place to begin. "Tamara's not in the picture, Corri. I haven't talked to her in months before tonight. Hell, I don't even think about her anymore."

"She told me you were the one that ended the relationship. I was under the impression it might be the other way around."

He wasn't all that surprised Tamara had confronted Corri with that knowledge, but he hated like hell that he hadn't been able to intervene. "Our relationship wasn't going anywhere, and she knew that."

"Then you're confirming you were the one who broke it off?"

Aidan wasn't in the mood to get into this tonight. But if he didn't explain, he had almost no chance of having the evening end on a positive note. He rolled onto his side in order to measure her reaction. "When we met, Tamara was a staff writer at the network. I recognized she had talent—"

"I just bet you did."

He ignored Corri's cynicism and prepared to lay it all out, even if he'd prefer to use his mouth for something other than talking. "I recognized she was a talented *writer*, and I pulled some strings so she was first in line to replace the head writer when he left. After we started seeing each other, the situation wasn't good. It didn't take long to realize sex and office politics don't mix. That's when I decided to make the move and strike out on my own."

Corri frowned. "I thought you moved back home to be close to your parents."

"That played a part in my decision to locate the studio in Houston."

"And Tamara decided she didn't want to follow you."

This is where it became thorny. If he didn't watch his step, he could very well come off sounding like a jerk. Sounding like his brother. "I told her that once I was settled in, I'd find a place for her at the studio. Then I started to realize it wasn't going to happen for us."

"Did you bother to explain that to her?"

"In a manner of speaking." And he'd failed several times in getting his point across. "She tried to talk me into returning to New York, and by then I knew I didn't want to leave Texas. Long-distance relationships don't work." Particularly when he hadn't found sufficient motivation to work on a relationship that didn't stand a chance in hell of surviving, even if they had been in closer proximity.

"I'm sure it's liberating, having your own studio," she said. "Being your own boss."

Again he was moving onto shaky ground, but for some reason he felt the need to come clean to Corri after months of sustaining his usual silence. "It wasn't only about the freedom the studio provided me, Corri. Someone else caught my attention around the time I ended it with Tamara."

"Let me guess. It's that persistent woman, Janine. Or maybe her name was Joyce."

Time to lay the truth on the line, even if it might cost him in the long run. "It was you."

Corri could only recall two times in her life that she'd been rendered speechless—when her parents had told her about the divorce, and now.

"Don't look so surprised, Corri. You had to know that kiss last March wasn't an accident."

She hadn't let herself believe that, out of guilt. Out of fear. "Actually, I assumed it was just one of those things. Afterward, I felt so horrible, I put it out of my mind." Or at least she'd tried, until Aidan had successfully dredged up the memory. "According to Kevin, you and Tamara were practically married back then."

"Kevin was wrong. We never even talked about marriage. Two days after the party, I called it off with Tamara. I realized if I was that attracted to you, I wasn't ready to commit to her."

"And then Kevin and I came back into town engaged." Another prime instance of poor timing, the way it seemed to be going with her and Aidan.

He rolled onto his back and stared at the ceiling. "I regretted introducing you to Kevin. I hated like hell knowing that he was in your bed."

That couldn't have been as difficult as watching

Aidan with his former lover tonight had been, knowing that in fact they *had* shared a bed, whereas she and Kevin had not. But Aidan didn't know that truth yet, and she wasn't sure when, or even if she should tell him.

"He's never treated you well," he continued. "That's been obvious when you've shown up at the family get-togethers without him."

Had she not been so attached to Kevin's and Aidan's parents, she would never have attended those gatherings at all. Where his family life included close-knit siblings, hers had involved bitter divorce battles. That solid family unit had made the O'Briens very appealing. And now she would have to give that up, all because of the grave error she'd made when she'd become engaged to a man she hadn't loved.

On that thought, Corri prepared to ask the question that had been haunting her all evening, even though she wasn't sure which answer she wanted to hear—yes or no. "Did you love Tamara, Aidan?"

He sighed. "I'm not exactly sure what that means."

"I'm not sure, either." She was sure about one thing—if not careful, she might learn what it meant if she continued down this path with Aidan. "Where do we go from here?"

He traced the swell of her breasts. "I only know that I've waited months to be with you, but it's up to you if you want this to go any further."

And therein lay the dilemma for Corri. Did she dare continue this phase of their relationship and possibly be sorry later? Or did she end it now, knowing that Aidan could only offer her an affair. A sexual distraction. A great escape. But when he looked at her so seriously, and seemed so sincere, her defenses melted.

Corri rested a hand on his jaw. "No expectations beyond this weekend?"

He lifted her hand and kissed her palm. "One step at a time."

Before long, Aidan had his hands all over her again, and Corri realized all too well what the next step would be. And she intended to put her best foot forward.

Corri awoke the next morning to find Aidan had left the bed at some point. It was now nearing 8:00 a.m., and they still had several hours before the flight departed, which meant they might have time for a little more action.

She sat on the edge of the bed and rolled her eyes. In one night, Aidan O'Brien had turned her into a mean female sex machine. Parts of her ached from the activity, other parts craved more.

Right now she could take care of the sore spots with a nice hot bath, and at the same time rely on Aidan to tend to the rest, provided she convinced him to join her in a little water play. She probably wouldn't have to do all that much to convince him.

With that in mind, she crossed the room and rifled through her bag for the oversized T-shirt she'd brought along. After slipping it on, she walked into the living room to seek out her incomparable date for the weekend, but he wasn't anywhere in sight. She went back into the bedroom and found the bathroom door ajar, but no Aidan. Wherever he'd gone this morning, she hoped he'd come back soon. In the meantime, she planned to make good use of that mammoth whirlpool until he returned.

Aidan didn't particularly care to have this early-morning meeting, but if he ever hoped to have some peace, he had to get it over and done with. He strode into the coffee shop and after working his way through the patrons and harried wait staff, he spotted Tamara at a corner table near the window. As always, she didn't have a dark hair out of place and her tailored blue designer suit shouted money. Despite their less than friendly parting, he recognized she was still a beautiful woman, and at one time having her in his life had meant something to him. But not now. The only woman who held his interest was upstairs asleep in the bed he planned to return to—as soon as he had this unfinished business out of the way.

When he reached the table, Aidan pulled out the chair across from her and sat. "Let's make this quick, Tamara. I don't have a lot of time."

She smiled in spite of his impatient tone. "And good morning to you, too, Aidan."

When the waitress arrived with a pot of coffee, Aidan told her, "I need two cups to go." Heavy emphasis on "to go."

"Where's your friend this morning?" Tamara asked as soon as the waitress left. "Torri, isn't it?"

She knew damn well it wasn't. "Corri's still asleep."

"Late night, I presume. But then I'd expect nothing

less from you. I remember several times when we spent Sundays in bed, all day."

He wasn't in the mood for a trip down memory lane. "What did you want to talk to me about?"

"Actually, I needed to tell you something before you heard it from someone else." She held out her hand, displaying a diamond the size of Rhode Island. "I'm engaged."

Aidan waited for the bite of disappointment, for even a clue of jealousy. Neither came. "Congratulations. Anyone I know?"

"Cameron Farr."

One of the directors at the studio who had a reputation for womanizing. "I didn't realize the two of you were seeing each other."

She rested her elbow on the table and supported her cheek with her palm. "We've been dating about six months. I couldn't wait for you forever."

That's how long she would have had to wait. "I'm happy for you, Tamara. Good luck. Anything else?"

"As a matter of fact, yes." She sat back and folded her arms. "This Corri, is she special?"

More than she knew. More than Corri knew. "She's a great woman."

"Is it serious?"

"We're friends, Tamara. Any particular reason for the grilling?"

"Yes. Hal told me she's got a lot of potential, and that one of the cable networks is very interested in her."

Aidan wasn't surprised that his former colleagues were privy to that knowledge. Word traveled fast in the television industry, particularly when the powers that be intentionally started the buzz. "What's your point, Tamara?"

"Just a few words of advice, Aidan. Maybe it would be best for you to end it now, before you break her heart like you did mine."

He couldn't even consider doing that in the near future. "I never meant to hurt you, Tamara, but I couldn't force feelings that weren't there. That wouldn't have been fair to you."

She sighed. "I know. Someone always seems to love a little more, don't they?"

He didn't know because he realized now, more than ever, he'd never been in love. Not with Tamara. Not with any woman.

When the waitress returned with his coffee, he took a quick check of his watch, more from the desire to get back to Corri than true lack of time. "I need to go. Again, congratulations."

Tamara continued to study him as if trying to uncover some hidden secret. "You know something, Aidan. You look different. More relaxed. Maybe Corri is good for you. Maybe she's the one to finally break through that impenetrable emotional fortress you're so proud of."

"I'm out of here." Before he had to hear about his inability to express his feelings.

When he stood, Tamara said, "Now that would be ironic, *you* falling in love with your own special project. A woman who's going to leave you for a better career opportunity."

He tossed a ten on the table, picked up the paper cups

and left the restaurant without granting Tamara a response or another look. But he did give her comments some thought.

He'd worked hard to overcome several obstacles to get where he was today, and the studio needed to be his main focus. Corri was at the top of her game, and he had no right to keep her from realizing her potential. After all, Tamara had been right on several counts. He'd discovered Corri, and she would be known as another of his successes in the near future. Falling in love with her would definitely be irony at its finest, even if he had no intention of doing that. None whatsoever.

But as he walked into the crowded elevator, he felt as if he couldn't get back to her fast enough.

Six

"Did you use the whole bottle of bubble bath?"

Jarred from her soaking stupor by the deep tenor of Aidan's voice, Corri looked up to find him standing in the open door, leaning against the frame, a paper cup clasped in one hand. He looked like the answer to all her feminine fantasies—clean-shaven, immaculately combed hair, long-sleeved untucked black polo and jeans. He could walk right into a model shoot on the downtown New York streets without anyone questioning his presence. He could get into the tub with her and she wouldn't mind a bit.

Apparently she was quickly becoming a lost cause where he was concerned, and she needed to stop that now. Or in the next few hours or so.

Corri reached for the washcloth, lifted her leg from

beneath the bubbles and bathed her thigh. "I used only half the bottle." When she met his gaze, she noticed his eyes had definitely darkened. "Where have you been?"

"To get this." He stepped inside the room and set the cup on the vanity. "Coffee, two sugars, a lot of cream."

"Just how I like it." She leaned forward and bent her knees to her chest, her body still concealed by the snowy mounds.

Aidan took a seat on the second step leading to the whirlpool and pushed aside a random strand of hair that had fallen from the clip. "I know what else you like, too."

He'd proved that to her twice last night. "You were gone for quite a while. How many blocks did you have to walk to get a cup of coffee?"

"I went downstairs to the restaurant. I had to meet with someone."

Someone was rather vague. "Friend or former colleague?"

"Tamara."

"Oh." That one word held a world of disappointment that Corri couldn't conceal. "What did she want?" As if she didn't know. Most likely she'd been pleading her case for a reconciliation with Aidan.

"She wanted to tell me she's engaged."

That she hadn't expected. Things were suddenly looking up. "Why didn't she mention that last night?"

"Because I didn't ask her. I told her congratulations, and then I left. It took about ten minutes, tops."

Don't ask, Corri. "Were you disappointed to hear that?"

He shook his head. "Not in the least. Tamara deserves a man who can give her what she needs. I'm not that man."

Corri experienced a strong sense of relief, and also a touch of wariness. He might not be the man she needed, either. But she couldn't concern herself with that now.

She sank down into the bath and sighed. "I really wish I had one of these tubs. Talk about a stress reliever."

"I have one at my house."

"Really? I don't see you as a whirlpool kind of guy."

He drew a slow circle around her knee. "I'm not. Is the water still warm?"

"It's lukewarm."

He rubbed the inside of her thigh. "How about you?"

She was veritably steaming. "I'm getting warmer."

"Then why don't you get out and let me take of that."

"Why don't you get in?"

"I've already had a shower."

She folded her arms on the ledge and used them as a resting place for her chin. "I'll convince you that big bathtubs have big benefits."

He lowered his hand to his fly, drawing her complete attention. "I'm suddenly more than up for a bath."

When she noticed the prominent crest, her insides began to dissolve right along with the bubbles. Before she could say "three-layer raspberry chocolate cake," he had his clothes off and one foot balanced on the tub's ledge, giving her a stellar view of his equally stellar physique. "Make some room for me."

She sat forward, allowing him to climb in behind her. When he tugged her back against him, she encountered a very solid, very potent nudge at her back. She rolled over and slithered up his body. "Looks like someone brought a toy into the tub with him."

"And I'm more than willing to share it with you."

Corri slid her fingers down his firm belly and took his "toy" into her hands. She stroked and explored, caressed and coaxed until Aidan caught her wrist and brought her hand against his chest. "That's enough playing for now."

"You're no fun."

"That's not what you said last night. Now let's get you out of here and back into bed where we have more room to do this right."

She kissed him above his navel. "You don't think we can improvise?"

His smile arrived, but only halfway, with full effect. "We could, but the condom's in the other room."

And that was something Corri dared not forget— protection against pregnancy. "Next time, we need to be better prepared." Funny how "next time" had slid so easily from her mouth.

Corri stood first and tried to walk down the steps as gracefully as possible, not an easy accomplishment on the slippery surface. But at least her feet didn't fail her, although that was a distinct possibility when Aidan left the tub in all his masculine glory. Without warning, he grabbed her into his arms without allowing her to dry off. "We're getting everything wet, Aidan," she scolded as they left a soggy trail across the carpet on the way to the bed.

"I like you wet." He deposited her on the edge of the bed, stepped back and told her, "Take down your hair."

She removed the clip, set it on the nightstand next to the lone condom, then shook out her hair. "Better?"

He gave her a patently appreciative look. "Oh, yeah. Now up on the bed."

Corri stretched out atop the mangled sheets and rested her head on the pillow, while Aidan remained seated beside her. "Last night was great," he said. "But I rushed things too much. This morning, I'm going to take my time."

She agreed that both rounds of lovemaking had been hot and fast, but she hadn't minded at all. "We have to check out in a couple of hours." Was there no end to her inane comments? No one made love for two hours straight.

He traced a line from between her breasts to her navel with his fingertip. "I'll call for a late check-out if I have to. And I might have to."

Okay, so *she'd* never made love for two hours. But she had a feeling Aidan had. He started by touching her, by telling her how much he appreciated her body. He palmed her breasts and lowered his head to flick his tongue over her nipple, then the silver loop in her navel.

When he raised his head and took an up close and personal look at her in the bright light of day, Corri battled self-consciousness. She'd been blessed with a long waist and legs, but she'd always believed her hips were a bit too wide. Aidan didn't seem to mind at all, and he told her so. He worked his way down, streaming his palms along her legs and his lips over her body.

And so it went for long, lazy moments. He kissed places that had never been kissed—the bend of her knee, the tips of her toes, the tiny mole below her pelvic bone. He said things that no man had ever said to her. Most highly suggestive, some surprisingly complimentary.

And he didn't stop there. He moved between her parted legs, and following one sexy and somewhat devious smile, he lowered his head. He was terribly sinful and tender in turn. He knew exactly how far to go, and when to let up, and how to use the pull of his lips, the play of his fingertips inside her to full advantage.

Corri exhaled a ragged breath when the pressure began to build, and bit back the scream that tried to escape. She didn't scream during sex. She never had. She wasn't going to now. Oh, yes, she was. With all the strength she had left, she clamped her hand over her mouth and closed her eyes. Fortunately, the sound came out as a muffled groan when the orgasm took hold. Her back arched involuntarily, and still Aidan continued with his own brand of beautiful torture until he'd wrung out every last contraction.

Her respiration was so uneven, she sounded as if she could use a tank of pure oxygen. And when Aidan slid back up her body and whispered, "I hope you enjoyed that as much as I did," she thought of requesting CPR, at the very least. Aidan kissed her before moving away and draping his legs over the side of the bed to take care of the condom.

He regarded her over one shoulder. "Come here and stand in front of me."

Corri went to her knees and draped her arms around his neck from behind. "I know why you enjoy your job so much. You like telling people what to do."

"I'm good at what I do because I recognize natural talent. Now come here and show me yours."

Her excitement barely contained, Corri crawled from

the bed and once she was positioned before him, he clasped her hips and urged her forward. "I want you on top this time."

That thought alone nearly sent her into orbit. "Think you can handle it, O'Brien?"

"I can handle anything you've got."

When he inched back a little, she climbed onto the bed, her knees on either side of his thighs. He urged her forward and up, then guided himself inside her. The sensations were exquisite, and so were Aidan's eyes that he kept centered on her gaze. "Do your best, Corri."

She absolutely intended to do just that. With her hands planted firmly on his shoulders, she lifted her body slowly, then lowered herself even more slowly. She repeated the move several times, delighting in Aidan's grip tightening on her hips, the hard set of his jaw that indicated he was close to losing control. And that was fine by her. After all, he'd driven her past the point of restraint several times now, and in this instance, turnabout was fair play.

She picked up the pace, and Aidan picked that moment to tangle his hands in her hair and lower his mouth to her breast. After that, anything remotely resembling slow went straight out the twenty-first-floor window.

As if she'd turned into some wild she-cat, she nudged him onto his back, her hips still firmly in his grasp, his body still deep inside her. She relished her newfound power and his response to it. Watching the transformation from a man in charge to a man about to lose it was a wonder for Corri to behold, and an undeniable turn-on. Perspiration beaded his forehead as his chest rose and fell with each move she made. And then he clenched his teeth, closed his eyes, jerked his hips up and hissed out a jagged breath, bringing on Corri's own climax.

He wrapped his hand around the back of her head and brought her against his chest. She could hear the sound of his pounding heart, felt his body finally relax after a time.

"We're good together, Corri," he said as he stroked her hair in a soft, soothing cadence.

She lifted her head and smiled. "You think so?"

"You don't?"

Oh, she definitely did. But that was only about bodies in motion. Raw, uninhibited sex. And for the first time, she allowed herself to wish that it could be more.

He wished he had more time with her, but family obligations dictated he leave her on her second-floor apartment doorstep where they now stood.

Corri set her bag down near the door and wrapped her arms around his waist. "I had a great time, Aidan."

"So did I." Better than he could have begun to imagine.

"Do you want to come in for a while?"

He did, but he wouldn't. Not if he wanted to spare himself from having to explain why he hadn't shown up for the Christmas Eve dinner—because he couldn't get enough of his brother's ex-fiancée. "I'm already an hour late. When I called my mother from the airport, she said my nephew was ready to open the presents. Since he's only ten months old, I'm not sure how she knows that."

She smiled. "He's probably enamored of all the pretty paper. That's the way it usually is with babies."

He brought her in closer. "I didn't realize you had experience with kids."

"I bought my designer prom dress with babysitting money."

Another surprise among many where Corri was concerned. Considering their numerous conversations, he'd mistakenly believed he knew everything about her. He'd definitely seen a side of her last night and this morning that he hadn't known existed, proving once again that his brother was an idiot for turning her loose. And he'd liked what he'd discovered. "I'll call you tonight after I've talked with my parents."

She looked more than a little wary. "Okay. But only if it's a positive conversation." She shook her head. "Never mind. Call me even if it's bad news. That way I can be prepared when I eventually talk with them."

If the news was bad, he might deliver it personally. He might suggest that anyway, but then decided he should stay away from her until he could assess where this relationship was heading. But he wasn't going to leave without a kiss. He cupped her face in his palm and lowered his mouth to hers, intending to deliver something quick and simple. That didn't happen. By the time they finally parted, he was ready to say obligation be damned and back her right into her bedroom.

She patted his chest and stepped out of his arms. "You better go before Lucy sends out a posse to come looking for you. And I'm sure she wouldn't be too pleased to know you're with me."

"I'm not going to tell her. It's better if they don't know about us."

"You're right."

Aidan didn't like hiding their relationship, or the disappointment in her tone. "But it's going to be damned hard not to touch you tomorrow."

She frowned. "I haven't agreed to go yet."

He was going to make certain she went, somehow, someway. He didn't want her spending Christmas alone. He didn't care to spend the day without her. "We'll discuss it later, when I call you tonight."

She withdrew her keys from her pocket and smiled. "Have a good time, and give your family my regards."

"You can do that tomorrow."

Without waiting for her rebuttal, Aidan sprinted down the stairs and slid into his car before he reconsidered and followed her inside. As he turned the ignition, he looked up to see Corri standing at the railing, watching him. Dressed in a sweater and jeans, her blond hair blowing back from her face, she looked too tempting to ignore. But he had to ignore her, otherwise he'd never make it to the party.

He left the complex a little faster than he should have, and as he pulled onto the interstate and headed west, he battled the urge to turn around several times and go back to Corri, especially when he got tied up in a Christmas Eve traffic jam, thanks to last-minute shoppers. Right now he only wanted to get the festivities over with and get back home so he could call Corri, to report, he hoped, that all hell hadn't broken loose in the family.

"What are you doing here?" Corri was proud that she'd sounded so calm after she'd opened the door to find her ex-fiancé on her stoop. Old flames were leaping out of the woodpile at an alarming rate.

Kevin tried to look contrite, but it wasn't working on Corri. "Thought I'd drop by to say hi."

"Hi, Kevin. Now goodbye."

When she tried to close the door, he slapped his palm on the facing. "Come on, Corri. I just want a few minutes of your time before I have to catch a plane."

Seeing a golden opportunity to give him a piece of her mind, Corri stepped aside. "You have two minutes."

He walked into the apartment, stood in the middle of the living room and looked around. "I'm surprised Aidan's not here."

She folded her arms across her middle. "He's at your parents' house. Since you're obviously not in Aspen, why aren't you there?"

He shrugged. "I'm on my way, so I didn't really have time."

"But you had time to come here."

"In the spirit of the holidays, I decided I owe you an apology."

Corri expected the roof to cave in at any moment. "You're right. You do owe me an apology and an explanation. That was pretty low, Kevin, sending me a note after I spent months playing by your rules."

"I know. But I wanted to tell you that I appreciate what you've done for me, and I'm sorry it didn't work out between us."

He wasn't the least bit sorry, that much Corri knew. She suddenly felt tired and empty of the energy it would take to give him a lengthy cursing. "Fine, Kevin. It's done. Apology accepted." She gestured toward the front door. "You should probably catch that plane now."

"You're right."

Corri followed him onto the porch and catching her off guard, he gave her a brief but awkward hug. "Merry Christmas. I hope you have a good life."

Corri didn't feel any spark of longing, any hint of regret. She did experience an odd touch of fondness for Kevin since it seemed he was finally cultivating some character. "I wish you well, too, Kevin. I also hope you find someone to settle down with." To settle him down, although that seemed highly unlikely, at least in the near future.

He favored her with the grin that had once charmed her, but not any longer. "You know me, Corri," he said. "Footloose and fancy free suits me fine."

Oh, yes, she knew that about him. She also knew that someday, he would encounter a woman who would take him down a notch or two. She only hoped she was around to see it, even if that was improbable. "Have a safe flight, Kevin."

"Thanks." Hands in pockets, he turned toward the stairs and took a step before facing her again. "One more thing. I know I said you could keep it, but can I have the ring back? I haven't paid for it yet."

Her recently elevated opinion of him blew away on the cool winter breeze. "Fine. I'll get it."

On her way to the bedroom, Corri bit back a litany of words that would blister a stockpot, including a few suggestions on where he could insert the piece of jewelry. She retrieved the blue velvet box from her dresser drawer, and was immediately reminded of that unmemorable proposal he'd given her one night back in April.

Here, Corri. Wear this. It makes the engagement look more official.

Corri took the ring from the holder, left the box on the dresser, and went back to the front porch to find Kevin leaning against the rail.

"Here you go, Kevin. One diamond on loan." When she reached out to hand it to him, she purposely dropped the ring on the ground and watched it roll through the break in the railing where it would land in the hedge two stories down.

She momentarily covered her mouth with her hand and faked mortification. "Oops. How clumsy of me. Would you like to borrow a flashlight?"

Kevin narrowed his dark eyes and glared at her. "Thanks a lot, Corri. I hope you feel better now."

Actually, she did, even if she also felt a bit childish. But as he stormed down the stairs, she also felt somewhat vindicated. And to think for a few moments she'd almost felt sorry for him.

Corri walked back into the apartment, stretched out on the couch, and realized how glad she was to be rid of Kevin. In the meantime, she would patiently wait for a call from his brother—the man she was learning to appreciate more each day. The man she could easily love.

For almost four hours, Aidan had waited for the opportunity to speak with his parents alone. Now that his siblings and their significant others had left, he went in search of his mother in her usual place—the kitchen—

but found only his father seated at the round dinette, his massive frame dwarfing the ladder-back chair, as he consumed a large piece of Lucine Kabakian O'Brien's baklava. He remembered the day back in August when Corri had somehow managed to charm Lucy into giving her the secret recipe, something no one else outside the immediate family had ever been able to do. Aidan was counting on their close relationship to help smooth things over if necessary. He hoped like hell that it wouldn't be.

Aidan took the chair across from his dad and watched while his father ate the pastry with gusto. "Does your wife know you're having another piece?"

"No, and I'm not aiming to tell her." Dermot nudged the plate toward him. "Have some."

That was the last thing he wanted, more food. "No thanks. Where is Mother, anyway?"

"She went to bed early with one of her headaches."

Damn. Obviously he'd waited too long to have this conversation. "I needed to talk to her about tomorrow."

His dad wiped away the syrup from his mouth with a paper napkin, balled it up and then tossed it into the trash can across the room. "Don't be tellin' me you're not going to be here. Your ma's already upset that Devin has to work at the hospital and Stacy will be taking little Sean to her parents. And Kevin having to do that interview in Colorado on Christmas Day added to Corri breaking up with the boy, well, that's enough stress for my Lucine."

Damn Kevin's lies. "First of all, Kevin isn't working, he's in Aspen playing with the snow bunnies. Secondly,

Kevin ended the engagement, not Corri. And finally, I'll be here." With Corri in tow, something he would get around to in a while.

Dermot cocked his head to one side and studied Aidan with confusion. "You're sayin' Kevin broke up with our Corri?"

Our Corri. At least that was a good sign. "Yeah, Dad, he broke up with her, and he wasn't even man enough to face her. He wrote a letter."

Dermot slapped his palms on the table, rattling the plate, his face a ruddy red. "I'm beginning to think that lad is a right eejit. Has he been sayin' why he would do such a fool thing?"

Aidan knew why, but it wouldn't please his father. At the moment, he didn't care. "Kevin liked having her around to impress his cronies. And now that he has his promotion, he doesn't need her anymore."

"That must've broken the lassie's heart."

He opted to leave out the part about Corri going along with the ruse. "She wasn't that surprised by the breakup. She was upset that he didn't tell her in person. She deserved that much after the hell he's put her through."

"I take it you've been consolin' her."

"I've done what I can to help her get over it." More than he was willing to admit to his family, or anyone for that matter.

When Dermot cracked a wide grin, Aidan realized he'd said too much. "Why, son, I do believe you'd like to step right in and be her fella."

He should know not to try to put anything over on Dermot O'Brien. "I'm being her friend, Dad. That's what she needs right now, not a *fella*. I plan to bring her for Christmas lunch tomorrow."

Dermot rubbed a hand over the back of his beefy neck. "Do you think that's wise, son? I wouldn't want her to feel out of place."

"You're worried about Mother's reaction."

"You know how she fancies Kevin, son. She thinks that boy can do no wrong. As much as she likes Corri, Kevin is her flesh and blood and to hear him tell it, he's the one who's been shagged."

When, in fact, Kevin had engaged in more than his fair share of shagging. "Look, if you think it's going to upset Mother, I won't bring her."

"Bring her. I'll have a talk with your ma."

"Fine. Call me if you change your mind. I can always stop by here for a while, but I plan to spend the day with Corri."

Dermot narrowed his eyes. "You can't fool your old da, Aidan. You've had your sights set on that girl since last St. Paddy's when you had a meet with her in the kitchen."

"How the hell did you know about that?"

"We all know, Aidan, except for your ma. I wouldn't want her to be thinkin' less of Corri because one of her boys stole a kiss from his brother's girl."

Apparently everyone knew his business, and he didn't like that one damn bit. All the more reason not to add more fuel to the fire. "Like I've said, Dad, Corri and I are friends. That's all."

Dermot grinned again. "Sure, son. And my arse is made of gold."

Seven

When the phone rang, Corri nearly jumped out of her fuzzy zebra-striped slippers. After bolting from the sofa, she banged her shin on the coffee table in a sleep-induced haze and answered, "Hello," through gritted teeth.

"Did I wake you?"

The sound of Aidan's voice definitely woke her up. Every part of her. "I guess I must have drifted off during the cheesy movie I was trying to watch." She glanced at the clock on the wall. "It's almost midnight. Looks like the O'Briens had quite a party."

"Actually, I left about a half hour ago. I've been driving around."

She yanked up one leg of the flannel pajamas and checked her aching leg to find a nice welt. "Were you looking at holiday decorations?"

"I was thinking about you."

His voice was so low and sensual, she dropped the pajama leg and nearly dropped the phone. "Really? I've been thinking about having a bowl of mint chocolate chip ice cream." *Liar.*

"I just passed the exit to your apartment. I almost took it."

"Why didn't you?"

"I thought you probably needed your rest."

She wasn't certain if she would sleep much tonight, if at all. "Did you have a nice visit with the family?"

"Yeah."

"Well?"

"Well what?"

Frustrating man. "Did you speak with your parents?"

"I talked to my dad. Mother went to bed early with a headache."

"Then they know about the breakup?"

"They heard Kevin's version. I set them straight."

Corri wasn't sure she wanted to know Kevin's version, although she suspected he'd painted her as a wretched heartbreaker. "Do they hate me now?"

"Not at all. They want you there tomorrow."

"Are you sure, Aidan?"

"Positive. My dad said when you're not welcome, then his ass is made of gold, or something along those lines."

Corri laughed, as she often did when Dermot spewed his Irish words of wisdom. "I'm really looking forward to seeing them." Even if it might be the last time, at least in that setting.

"Then I'm not going to have to pick you up and

throw you over my shoulder in order to get you out of the apartment?"

"Although that sounds very interesting, I promise to go willingly." She hesitated a moment before blurting, "Speaking of apartments, guess who showed up at mine tonight?"

"I don't have a clue."

"Kevin."

A moment of dead silence passed before Aidan said, "I'm turning around."

"Aidan, I'm fine. You don't have to—"

The cell phone clicked off before Corri had the opportunity to finish her protest. Granted, she wouldn't mind seeing Aidan. She'd absolutely love it, in fact. But she didn't want him to assume she was broken up over his brother's impromptu visit. He shouldn't feel that he had to ride to the rescue every time she mentioned the word *Kevin*.

When he arrived, she planned to set him straight, let him know that although she appreciated it, his concerned was misplaced.

A few minutes later, the doorbell rang and nervous anticipation shot Corri straight off the sofa to answer the summons. She slipped on her robe en route and opened the door to find Aidan leaning against the railing where Kevin had stood a few hours ago. "I only want to know one thing," he said in his I-mean-business voice. "Why was Kevin here?"

"He wanted to apologize, if you can believe that."

His somber expression told her he didn't. "Kevin doesn't apologize for anything."

"Okay, he really wanted the ring back, the one he told me I could keep. I let him have it, and he left."

"That's all he wanted?"

Never in a million years had Corri believed Aidan would sound so jealous. "Why? Do you think we had a quick roll for old times' sake?"

"Did you?"

That had been the last thing on her mind. "No, we did not."

He came away from the railing and took two stalking steps toward her before pulling up short. "Tell me something. Do you compare me to him when we're in bed together?" When she failed to speak, Aidan moved closer. "Answer me, Corri."

She now had the perfect moment to tell the truth. To finally set the record straight. To let him know that her relationship with his brother had never entered into that realm. "Kind of hard to make a comparison when I've never made love with Kevin."

Aidan looked taken aback before the surprise dissolved into disbelief. "You're telling me that in nine months' time, not once did you and Kevin have sex."

Corri pulled her robe tighter to ward off the cold, and the bitterness brought about by the memories. "In Jamaica, he came into my room one night and crawled into bed with me. He'd been out drinking, so before anything happened, he passed out. After that, things were awkward between us, and Kevin found what he needed from other women. End of story."

He mulled that over for a minute before saying, "I've

always known my brother sometimes lacks in good judgment, but I never thought he was that stupid."

"Well, now you know. Anything else you'd like to interrogate me about?"

"That's it."

"We could have had this conversation over the phone, Aidan."

"True, but then I couldn't have done this." He was on her fast, bringing her up against him, kissing the very life out of her. But it didn't last long enough before he broke all contact and moved away.

When her head stopped reeling, Corri pointed behind her. "Do you want to come in?"

"Yes, but I'm not going to. The way I'm feeling right now, I'd have you awake all night, and you need some sleep. Otherwise, we'll be late for Christmas lunch."

As far as she was concerned, that might be worth a little tardiness. "You could say you had to change a flat tire."

He inclined his head and narrowed his eyes. "That's a tempting suggestion, but I'm going to wait until tomorrow night. And believe me, Corri, I'm going to give you a holiday you won't forget."

On the drive to the O'Brien's house the following morning, Aidan kept touching Corri—subtle strokes over her thigh, along her jaw, down her throat where the thin black sweater concealed her breasts. And Corri kept insisting that if he didn't stop it, she would be in no shape to act normally around his family.

Yet he didn't seem to care, and that was all too apparent when he stopped at the end of the block and kissed her soundly. "A prelude to tonight," he told her before finally pulling into the drive behind Dermot's ancient truck. After they gathered the gifts they'd brought with them, Corri walked up the path first, with Aidan maintaining a good distance behind her. The pretense had begun—again.

When Corri stepped inside the living room, she was struck by the hominess of the surroundings, from the beautiful decorated fir in the corner to the scents of baking bread wafting in from the nearby kitchen—everything she'd never had while growing up.

Mallory O'Brien Manning doled out the first greeting, followed by a hug. "I'm so glad you came, Corri," she said. "And I'm so sorry about Kevin's antics."

Corri handed off the bag of presents to Aidan, and continued to clutch the plastic container housing the desert she'd prepared. "Don't apologize, Mallory. It's over and done."

She then exchanged hellos with Aidan's two younger brothers, Logan, with the near-black hair and crystal blue eyes, and Kieran, leaving the oldest of the six children unaccounted for. When she inquired about Devin, Logan said, "He's the on-call resident at the hospital. Stacy took Sean to her parents' house, which is why we were here last night. You should have come over last night, too."

Corri wished she had, then maybe she could have avoided the little visit with Kevin. "Honestly, I still had to wrap presents. I tend to procrastinate."

Dermot came barreling into the room, gave Corri a tight hug and Aidan a hard slap on the back. "Good you two could make it." He eyed the container. "What fine fare have you brought us today, lassie?"

"My special pecan sugar cookies. I know how much Lucy likes them. Is she in the kitchen?"

"Where else would she be?" Dermot said. "Would you like me to take those to her?"

She shook her head. "I'll do it. I'll see if she needs a hand with the cooking." Sooner or later, she would have to face the woman who had once been her prospective mother-in-law. The woman who championed her one-time fiancé. Might as well get it over with.

"Let me know if you need any help, Corri."

She turned to find Aidan standing nearby and recognized he hadn't meant "help" as in with meal preparation. "I'm sure the two of us can handle it fine."

Mallory stepped up and asked, "Are you sure I can't do anything?"

"You need to sit and relax while you can, Mallory. Just think, this time next year, you'll have not one, but two babies to care for."

Mallory's husband, Whit, groaned, prompting laughter from the group—except for Corri. She didn't feel all that jovial, considering what she needed to do in the next few moments. "I'll be back in a while," she said, then headed toward Lucine O'Brien's inner sanctum, the place where the revered matriarch had prepared numerous dinners for her family for almost forty years. The place where Corri had joined her in making those dinners several times over the past few months.

Corri found Lucy standing by the sink, peeling yams for the traditional sweet potato casserole. She'd pulled her salt-and-pepper hair back into a low bun, and she wore a red and green festive sweater over her black slacks. She was still a beautiful woman, and she'd definitely passed her looks onto her children.

Corri set the container on the counter and said, "Smells great."

Lucy only afforded her a brief glance before going back to her chores. "Hello, Corinna."

Lucy never called her "Corinna." Not a good sign at all. "What can I do to help?"

Lucy paused with the vegetable peeler in mid-stroke. "Nothing. I have everything under control."

Lucy had never refused her help. Not once. Now Corri felt totally disheartened. "We need to talk, Lucy."

"About what?"

"About mine and Kevin's breakup."

"There's nothing to say, Corinna. It's done."

Corri took a chance and moved beside her. "I just want to say how sorry I am it didn't work out. I know how hard it was on you when Logan and Helena called off their wedding at the last minute, and now this."

Lucy sighed. "Young people today do not take their commitments seriously."

That sounded like an indictment to Corri, but she didn't feel she should argue the point. "I suppose that's true in some cases. But it's probably better to discover incompatibility before you take the vows."

When Lucy didn't respond, Corri laid a hand on her shoulder. "I also want you to know that regardless of what happened between Kevin and me, you'll always have my respect. I appreciate everything you've done for me, welcoming me into your home, making me feel a part of a real family for a little while. That means more than you know."

Lucy's eyes filled with tears right before she tossed the peeler into the sink, wiped her hands on a dish-towel, then rushed out of the kitchen.

Corri didn't try to stop her, but she did know one thing. She should never have come here today, and she had to get away.

The minute Corri bypassed the living room and headed out the front door, Aidan realized he should have accompanied her to confront his mother, whether she wanted him there or not. When he stood and strode into the entryway to go after her, Mallory rushed in front of him and blocked his path. "Let's give her a few minutes to herself."

Aidan streaked a hand over the back of his neck. "This is my fault. I should've known Mother would have a problem with Corri showing up."

"I'll talk to Corri, and you go talk to Mother," Mallory said. "She'll listen to you."

"Not when it involves Kevin."

"You owe it to Corri to try, otherwise this holiday's going to be ruined for both of them."

Aidan had to agree. He only hoped he wasn't too late to salvage the situation. "I'm not sure I'll get anywhere."

"All you can do is try, Aidan."

He turned around then reconsidered and faced his sister again. "Don't wait too long to check on Corri."

She saluted. "Yes, sir, Captain O'Brien. And you

don't wait too long to own up to the fact that you care about Corri more than you're willing to admit. To her, and to yourself."

Aidan had no desire to get into that with Mallory, or no readily prepared denial. Right now he had to smooth things over with his mother. If that didn't work, then he'd take Corri out of here and spend his holiday with her at his house.

When he didn't find Lucy in the kitchen, he walked the hallway to the master bedroom, where he found his dad seated on the edge of the mattress, his arm around Lucy's back. Aidan could tell his mother had been crying, and as bad as that made him feel, he couldn't ignore the bite of anger. She was too wrapped up in Kevin to realize she'd raised a son who didn't give a tinker's dam about anything aside from his job, or anyone, including Corri.

"Give us a few minutes, Dad," Aidan said, garnering their full attention.

Dermot scowled. "Whatever you might be tellin' my bride, son, I have a right to hear it, too."

"Fine." Aidan moved in front of them, leaving very little space between him and the bureau at his back.

The bureau.

Thinking about that while trying to talk to his parents about Corri wasn't a good idea. After driving the images from his mind, he cleared his throat and reined in his temper.

"Look, Mother, I know you had your hopes set on Corri and Kevin staying together, but it wasn't going to happen. Kevin's treated her like a jerk for nine months."

Lucy's red-rimmed brown eyes turned hard from anger. "I will not listen to you criticize your brother, Aidan."

"Yes, Mother, you sure as hell will listen." When Dermot started to speak, Aidan held up his hand to silence him. "Corri's a remarkable woman, and Kevin's too self-absorbed to see it. He cut her loose, and she's here with me today because she's a good friend. She's been a good friend to everyone in this family, including you both."

Lucy lowered her head and worked the hem on her apron. "Yes, but—"

"There are no buts in this situation. I expect you to get over it so we can all move forward. And if you can't be nice to her, then say the word, and I'll take her out of here, but I won't be coming back today."

His parents exchanged a glance, before Lucy said, "Then it's true, Aidan? You did kiss her back in March?"

That one kiss from months ago kept coming back to bite him on the ass. "What does that have to do with anything?"

Lucy brought out her grave motherly expression, the one that used to silence all of them when they were kids. "It's the reason you're defending her, Aidan. The reason she's here today. I can't help but wonder if there's more to your relationship with her. Perhaps you've been part of the problem between her and Kevin."

Aidan kept a tight rein on his anger, but barely. "I had nothing to do with Kevin breaking it off with Corri. Now you tell me what your answer's going to be. Corri's welcome and she stays, or she's not and we both leave."

Lucy's swiped a hand across her damp cheeks. "I'm not angry with Corri. I'm disappointed. I so wanted to have her for my daughter-in-law, and now that's not going to be possible."

Dermot tipped her head against his shoulder and stroked her cheek. "Don't worry, my love. These things have a way of working themselves out." He sent Aidan a wink. "Why, only last night, I told the lad here that if one looks hard enough, he might find gold right where he sits."

Lucy lifted her head and stared at them both. "You men speak in riddles." She regarded Aidan again. "Tell Corri she's welcome here. And also tell her that I could use some help with the meal. She's so gifted in the kitchen."

She had a lot of gifts neither of his parents knew about, and Aidan wasn't about to make any more revelations. "I'll tell her."

If she hadn't started the walk back to her apartment.

When she heard the door open behind her, Corri expected to look back from her perch on the cement step to find Aidan. Instead, Mallory walked onto the porch, her hands on her distended belly. She lumbered toward Corri and lowered herself beside her. "Did Mother give you a hard time?" she asked.

Although the temperature was in the mid-sixties, Corri felt chilled to the marrow thinking about the uncomfortable confrontation. "It's not her fault. My coming here was a bad idea."

"No, it wasn't, Corri. No matter what happened with you and Kevin, you're still a family friend. Mother needs time to adjust. She loves you, and that's why she's so upset. That and the fact that her favorite son didn't bother to show up for Christmas. Again."

Corri wondered if Lucy had assumed she had something to do with that. "I feel terrible, Mallory. I don't know how to explain to her what happened with Kevin. That the whole engagement was a…" *Lie.* She didn't have the energy to get into that right now. "It should never have happened."

"I've known that for months, Corri. I've also known that one O'Brien brother would be more than willing to step in and take Kevin's place, if he hasn't already."

She glanced at Mallory to find her smiling. "Did Aidan mention something about us?"

"He didn't have to say a word. I've seen the way he looks at you. The way he's always looked at you. He's totally, unequivocally in love with you."

Almost an exact replay of her conversation with Kieran. "He's not in love with me, Mallory. Lust maybe, but not love."

"Then the two of you are sleeping together?"

She saw no use in denying it to Mallory. The heat creeping up her neck to her face was a dead giveaway. "Yes, but that's only been very recent." All of two days ago. "Not once did Aidan ever make any overtures while Kevin and I were together."

"Except for the kiss in the kitchen."

Apparently that had made the annual family newsletter without Corri's knowledge. "You know about that, too?"

"Logan told Whit, and Whit told me. But don't worry. I'm not going to make an announcement. I am going to have to go back inside in a few minutes since one of these girls is playing kickball with my bladder."

"I understand. And if you don't mind, could you ask Aidan to come outside for a minute?"

"I practically had to sit on him so he'd let me talk to you first."

Corri reached over and squeezed Mallory's hand. "Thanks for listening."

"You're welcome, and now you listen to me." Mallory shifted slightly to face Corri. "Aidan has a difficult time expressing his emotions, and although he would never, ever tell you this, his reticence comes from being a really quiet little kid."

Corri frowned. "Are we talking about the same Aidan? The man who commands attention every time he speaks?"

Mallory gave her auburn hair a one-handed sweep back from her face. "I know, it's hard to believe with this loud-mouth family, and the fact that he's quite the business negotiator now. But Aidan was very introverted. I always thought of him as the observer, the intuitive listener. When he reached high school, he suddenly blossomed into this gorgeous hunk. He was smart, athletic and one of the most popular guys in school. And still aloof, but the girls considered all that mystery very appealing. And he quickly learned to use that to his advantage."

Corri knew that first-hand. "All he had to do was crook a finger, and they came running, right?"

"He didn't have to do a thing but stand there. I remember when I was in junior high, and Aidan was a senior, girls called at all hours of the night. Of course, the conversations were brief. Something like 'Meet me Friday after the game in the parking lot.'"

Corri and Mallory shared a laugh before Mallory took on a serious expression. "I'm telling you this, Corri, to let you know that even if he hasn't told you what he's feeling yet, that doesn't mean he's not feeling it. I'd wager he will eventually come clean, if you give him time. Unless you don't have the same feelings for him."

Corri rested her chin on her bent knees. "I don't know how I feel. I only know that when I'm with him, I'm happier than I've been with any man. And that isn't about sex. That's about camaraderie and friendship."

"Take my word for it, Corri. There is nothing wrong with falling in love with your friend. I'm living proof."

That comment came as no surprise to Corri. Mallory had fallen for her roommate, and now they were happily married. But Corri couldn't see the wisdom in falling in love with a commitment avoider like Aidan.

She leaned over and gave Mallory a quick, heartfelt hug. "I appreciate the advice."

Mallory hoisted herself up from the step and planted a palm against her lower back. "And I'd appreciate February getting here fast so I can have these babies."

The door opened again and this time Aidan stepped onto the porch. On her way back inside, Mallory paused and patted her brother on the cheek. "Be good to her, Aidan."

When Mallory disappeared, Aidan joined Corri on the step. "Are you okay?"

She shrugged. "Not really. I think you should take me home before I upset your mother even more."

He draped an arm around her shoulder. "I had a talk

with her, and she's fine. She asked me to ask you if you mind helping her with the meal."

Corri gave him a wide-eyed look. "That's quite a turnaround from her earlier attitude."

"She's disappointed that you're not going to be a permanent member of the family. But you're still welcome here."

"Are you sure?"

"Would I lead you astray?"

She couldn't hold back her smile. "That depends. You've been trying to do that for the past few days."

"And you came along willingly."

"Yes, I did." Several times, in fact.

He leaned over and whispered, "Now come back into the house so we can get this over with. I still have to give you my gift, and I can't do it while the family's watching."

Aidan's deep, persuasive voice, the suggestion in his tone, the fire in his eyes, wrapped Corri in a blanket of warmth. "Well, now that you put it that way…"

Eight

As Aidan pulled away from the curb, Corri took a long, wistful look at the O'Brien family gathered together on the porch, waving goodbye. She felt as if this could be the last time she would be viewing this particular scene.

Her thoughts turned to the day's events as Aidan navigated the rural streets. She and Lucy had exchanged apologies and hugs, but she still had the strongest feeling that Lucy blamed her for the breakup, and in many ways she *was* to blame. If only she had put an end to the lies much sooner, before she'd become so emotionally involved with the family. Before she had to experience a final goodbye.

After realizing they were heading in the wrong direction, Corri sent a glance Aidan's way. "This isn't how you get to my apartment."

He reached over, caught her hand and laid it on his thigh. "I know. We're going to my place and I'll drop you back at your apartment in a few hours. I'd offer to let you spend the night and drive you to work in the morning, but that might cause more speculation."

Which basically meant they were having a typical covert affair, a few hours of stolen time. They couldn't tell Aidan's family. They couldn't be obvious at work. And regardless of what Aidan had said to her in New York—he didn't care what anyone thought—that wasn't accurate. And here she was again, hiding the truth about another relationship, only the truth was, being with Aidan had meant more to her than she'd ever expected.

And that's why she would enjoy whatever time they had together tonight, and decide what to do about everything tomorrow. She still had her work to fall back on, a nice place to land should she determine that a continuing relationship with Aidan might be detrimental to her heart.

By the time they reached Aidan's house, the sun had begun to set and the streets were dotted with assorted holiday lights. Several cars lined the streets, indicating the celebration still continued for some—and hopefully for Corri.

Once they were inside Aidan's den, he set the bags filled with gifts on the sofa table and said, "Wait here," then disappeared down the lengthy corridor that she had yet to explore.

Corri wandered around the room, thinking it odd that neither she nor Aidan had bothered to decorate for the holidays. She hadn't really seen the point in purchasing a tree, since traditions only fueled her loneliness when she had no one with whom to share them.

Just when Corri had decided she might have to go looking for him, Aidan reappeared. If she'd had any doubts about what he had planned, they were dispelled the minute she caught sight of his attire—a pair of low-slung jeans and nothing else. His chest was beautifully bare, his belly remarkably ridged, and his hair sensually tousled.

Mallory had been right about his effect on women. He didn't have to do a thing but stand there before he had Corri wanting to crawl all over him.

She folded her arms across her midriff and sized him up. "Looks like someone has a head start on me."

"Not for long."

Corri clasped his offered hand and followed him down the hallway, past three closed doors and a room that appeared to be a study. Beyond that, they took an immediate right and came face to face with an open set of double doors that revealed an enormous room. The king-size bed, draped in black, was set against one wide wall that soared all the way to vaulted ceiling. Contemporary pieces of art were set about the room, and when Aidan guided her inside, Corri felt as if she'd entered a world that was beyond her imagination.

"Wow." All she could think to say at the moment.

"You haven't seen the best part yet," he said as he let go of her hand and opened another set of double doors.

When Aidan stepped aside, Corri entered an opulent bathroom that didn't remotely resemble anything she'd ever seen. The double black vanities spanned one side, and set in the corner was a huge, transparent shower containing multiple faucets, with mirrored walls taking up the remaining space. But the most impressive focal point was centered in the room—a phenomenal tub surrounded by black marble steps on every side, and lined with candles. Lots and lots of candles that washed the area in a golden glow and exotic scents. When she spotted two condoms resting on one ledge, she realized he hadn't forgotten one detail, and her body reminded her how little it took to respond to him as he came up behind her and circled his arms around her waist.

"How do you like my whirlpool?" he asked.

"That's not a whirlpool, Aidan. That's a swimming pool."

His laugh was low and deep. "The builder was into the whole Roman-bath thing."

The builder was brilliant, Corri decided. "It's a beautiful bathroom, although I'm not sure how much I like all these mirrors. Talk about highlighting your body's flaws when you leave the shower."

He feathered a kiss across her cheek. "You don't have any flaws."

She started to point them out before reconsidering and turning into his arms. "You've really surprised me with the candles. I didn't see you as a romantic kind of guy."

"I promised you a holiday you wouldn't forget."

She had no doubt she would never forget it or him, no matter what the future held. "What now?"

"You're going to take a bath, and I'm going to return a couple of calls."

"Business-related?"

"Yes."

She feigned a pout. "And you're going to leave me here all by myself?"

"Did you have something else in mind?"

The man was teasing her, taunting her. That didn't mean she had to give in. Yet.

She pulled her sweater over her head and dropped it onto the carpeted floor. "Go ahead and take care of business." She toed out of her shoes, slid her jeans down then stepped out of them. "I'll have a good long soak while you do that."

He raked his gaze down her body and back up again. "I'll try not to be too long."

She unclasped her bra and tossed it onto the pile. "Why? Did *you* have something else in mind?"

He ran a hand down his abdomen, drawing her attention to the noticeable ridge below his fly. "What do you think?"

"I think you'd better hurry." She slipped her panties away and there she stood, completely naked while Aidan remained planted in the same spot. "Your phone calls are waiting," she said when he failed to move.

He backed up a few steps, all the while keeping his gaze trained on her body. "You're trying to distract me."

"I'm trying to take a bath." She sat on the second step leading to the tub, reached back and pressed the button that sent the jets whirling into action.

"Enjoy yourself." He flipped on a switch near the door, filling the room with the soft sounds of jazz. Then he was gone, which demonstrated his strength of will.

Corri climbed into the bath, lifted her hair and reclined against the towel strategically placed on the edge. As the whirlpool soothed her body, she considered all the money she'd wasted at the day spa when she could have used Aidan's tub. She also considered she could get used to frequent visits to this luxurious house, and with the house's owner. No, she couldn't. She had to keep in mind that this extended holiday, a vacation from reality, was only a temporary respite. Too much was still up in the air with their relationship, and she refused to set herself up for another fall.

Corri closed her eyes and cleared her mind. She was bent on enjoying the bath until Aidan returned. The swirling water, the soft strains of the music, lulled her into a drowsy state, and she began to drift off....

The sensation of something sliding against her skin forced her eyes open, and when she looked down, she truly thought she was caught in an incredible dream. A marquis-cut ruby, surrounded by a halo of diamonds, dangled from a gold chain between her breasts.

Corri straightened and looked back to find Aidan seated on the ledge behind her, smiling. "What is this for?" she asked.

"It's for you. Merry Christmas."

Unbelievable. "But I only got you a tie. And it wasn't even a serious tie. It has bats and baseballs on it and—"

He stopped her rant with a lingering kiss before pulling away and tracing the chain with a fingertip. "It looks good on you. As I said the other night, red's definitely your color."

"It's beautiful, Aidan. But it's really too much."

"I wanted to do it."

"I'm really glad you did." She sent him a coy smile.

"Why don't you climb in here with me and let me thank you properly."

He tested the water with one hand. "It's almost cold. Why don't you get out and thank me properly?"

"I suppose I could do that."

While Corri left the tub, Aidan held out a towel which he wrapped her in like a cocoon. She glanced in the mirror behind him and only then realized he was unabashedly naked. She was entirely turned on by the sight of his fabulous butt, the backs of his toned thighs. So much so that she simply had to touch. Working her arms from beneath the towel, she reached behind him and ran her hands over his back and kept going until she had both palms on his bottom.

The towel dropped, and so did Aidan's guard when he kissed her thoroughly with a stimulating sweep of his tongue. As he turned his attention to her neck, Corri could see all the details of his body, and hers in various angles, compliments of the mirrors, which gave the illusion that the room was much larger. Maybe this was all only an illusion: the extravagant necklace dangling at her throat, watching Aidan's hands roam over her while experiencing the heat of his touch—and the low sound of his voice at her ear when he said, "I can't get enough of you."

But her need for him was very real, and so was the absolute fire surging through her when he brought her down onto the plush black mat at the base of the tub. Again she had an unencumbered view in the mirror's reflection when he drew her breasts into his mouth, when he kissed his way down her body, when he brought her to a searing climax that left her weak and completely winded. She was only mildly aware that he'd left to retrieve the condom, but very aware when he eased inside her, then pushed deeper and deeper.

Yet this time something was different. This time their lovemaking was slower and surprisingly tender. Aidan held her face in his palms, kissed her softly, kept his gaze connected with hers. For a moment she thought he might say something, but then he quickened the cadence of his movements. For a split second she thought she might say something, too. Reveal the feelings she could barely own, much less voice. She was only one step ahead of falling in love with him, and that emotion was gaining ground so quickly it made her head spin. She couldn't even think about that now, not when she experienced the beginnings of another climax, the awareness that Aidan was on the verge as well. She allowed all her concerns to float away as he lifted up on straight arms, and with one more thrust, sent her over the edge with him.

They remained entwined right there on the bathroom floor, the sound of their labored breaths echoing in the room while a disturbing thought echoed in Corri's brain.

She'd already taken the fall. She was in love with him, lock, stock and barrel, and she couldn't do a thing about it. But she could finally acknowledge what she had purposely denied for months—she'd been in love with him since that kiss in the kitchen.

For the second time in two days, Aidan had Corri in his bed. He couldn't remember a time in the past year when he'd spent two nights with one woman. He'd never been in this place, either, waging a war with feelings that he'd never planned to have. Wanting her body was one thing. Wanting more than an affair was another thing altogether. Corri was balanced on the brink of stardom, and in a few weeks' time, if not sooner, she'd be leaving for a better opportunity. For that reason, he'd be damned if he let his emotions rule his head. Literally damned.

But right now, with her back fitted perfectly against his front, their hands laced together below her breasts, he didn't care about tomorrow or the next day or the next. Tonight was about all the future he could handle.

"Tell me something I don't know about you, Aidan."

I care about you more than you know jumped into his brain. "What do you mean?"

She glanced back at him and smiled. "You know, things we've never talked about, like your greatest fear."

"Fear is a counterproductive emotion." Although at the moment he feared she was close to breaking down a few walls he'd prefer to remain intact.

"Everyone's afraid of something," she said. "I'm personally afraid of bad ratings. Oh, and escalators."

"Escalators?"

"My dear mother. When I was about five, she told me a story about a kid getting chewed up by one because his shoestrings were untied. It was either avoid escalators from that point forward, or avoid cross-trainers. And since I like to work out, I chose escalators."

"Why did you choose culinary school?"

"I like stirring things up."

He palmed her breast with one hand. "So do I."

"No kidding." She rolled over to face him. "Why did you choose the broadcasting field?"

Territory he didn't care to enter. "I watched a lot of news growing up."

"Seriously."

"I am serious. At one time I thought about being a newscaster, but then I realized I was better suited to working behind the scenes."

She ran a fingertip along his collarbone. "Mallory told me you used to be shy."

Damn Mallory's open-book mentality. "I was more of a deep thinker and less of a talker. It used to amaze me when people opened their mouths without giving their brains time to work."

She lowered her forehead against his chest. "You've just described me."

He tipped her chin up and forced her to look at him, hating the hurt in her eyes. "That was an isolated incident, Corri. You lost control one time, and with good reason."

"Believe me, it's not the only time. Every time I'm with you, I seem to lose control."

"So do I, and I'm not sorry."

Her smile was hesitant. "Are you sure?"

He needed to find something to say to reassure her. "I want you to stay with me tonight, all night."

She frowned. "What about work tomorrow?"

"I'll take you to your apartment, which means we'll have to get up earlier than I'd planned. Then again, we might be up all night."

* * *

After being up a good deal of the night, Corri climbed out of bed at dawn and headed for her salvation—caffeine. She brewed a pot of coffee and took two cups back into the bedroom to find Aidan still sleeping. She set his cup on the nightstand and perched on the edge of the bed, one leg curled beneath her. Some time during the night, he'd turned onto his back, the position he maintained now with both hands resting loosely on his lower abdomen where the sheet covered the intimate terrain she knew so well. Dark whiskers blanketed his jaw, and a lock of hair fell over his brow. His eyes were tightly closed, his features slack, his lips pursed together. He shouldn't look so sexy, yet he did. The least he could do was snore. Anything to discourage her. But he didn't make a sound as his chest rose and fell in a steady rhythm.

Right as she was considering crawling back in bed to utilize some very creative and questionable ways to wake him, his eyes drifted open.

He rubbed his palm up his chest and back down again. "What time is it?"

Time for her to gather her wits before she ditched the caffeine and jumped him. "Almost seven."

"You're wearing my shirt."

Something she'd always imagined doing, but never had before. Then again, she'd done a lot of things with Aidan she'd never done before. "I found it in that garage-size closet in the bathroom. Hope you don't mind."

He reached out and slid his fingers beneath the tailored hem resting on her thigh. "I like you better without it."

She batted his hand away. "If you start anything now, we'll both be late. You still have to take me to my apartment."

He stacked his hands behind his head. "You're right."

In many ways she wished he would protest a little more, but she wouldn't be able to resist him if he did.

Now seemed like a good time to ask the question that had been gnawing at her all night, when he hadn't been touching her and she'd actually been able to think. "Since you own the studio, and you're the boss, explain to me exactly why it would be so terrible if people knew we were seeing each other?"

He turned his attention to the ceiling. "Because everyone feels the burn, Corri, from the crew on up to the studio executives. People will either come to you with their problems, thinking you can wield influence over me. Or they'll treat you like a pariah for fear you'll run and tell if they have any complaints."

That made sense, but not everything about their relationship did. "Then why even bother getting involved with me?" When he didn't respond, she said, "Well?"

He leveled his gaze on hers. "What do you want me to say?"

She shrugged. "I don't know. Maybe something like this thing between us doesn't account for logic. That you couldn't help yourself."

"All of that is true."

"How long are we supposed to pretend?"

He scooted up and reclined against the headboard. "Like I've said before, we'll take it one step at a time."

Coffee in hand, she left the bed, feeling a sudden urge to flee. "I'll get my clothes and get dressed."

As she crossed the room toward the bath, he called her name. When she faced him, he asked, "Are you okay?"

"I'm fine, Aidan."

As fine as anyone who realized that the man she cared for way too much was counting on the fire between them to die, as it most surely would, at least for him. And in the process, no doubt she would be the one to get burned.

She'd gone home in a cab yesterday morning, leaving only a note of thanks behind. She'd sequestered herself in the dressing room to prepare for the taping, and Aidan hadn't seen her all day. She hadn't bothered to pick up the phone when he'd called her last night, either.

He realized she was putting some distance between them, and he should be okay with that. But he wasn't. Not in the least.

And now he stood in the control booth, watching her walk onto the stage to a standing ovation with intrinsic grace, wearing his favorite red apron and a smile designed to make everyone take notice, especially the men. Aidan definitely noticed that, and everything about her. Today she wore her blond hair down around her shoulders instead of in her usual ponytail, and he briefly wondered if she was trying to make him suffer. If so, it was working. As badly as he hated to admit it, he'd missed her yesterday and last night. And this morning. He'd set a dangerous course, and if he knew what was good for him, he'd end it right now, before someone at the studio got wind of it, and the trouble began. For once in his life, he couldn't consider his work, only what he wanted. He wanted her, until circumstances sent them down different paths, as he knew they would.

Corri started the taping by giving the audience a self-deprecating speech on her behavior during the last show, along with an apology that garnered more applause. She moved through the script without a hitch, went through the motions of preparing a sensual meal to ring in the new year. When she caught his glance during the question-and-answer session, she faltered slightly, something Aidan had never known her to do before. A real pro, though, Corri recovered quickly.

She presented another bright smile and ended the show with, "If you can't be with the one you love, then love the food you're with." A slogan that would become her trademark. Something she could carry with her throughout her career. And after the call he'd received this morning, he realized she could be making a move that would end this thing between them, once and for all.

"That's a wrap," Parker said, then shook his head. "She's absolutely amazing. Did you see how the audience hung on her every word?"

Aidan had seen, and he needed to see her now. He had to know what was wrong, although he suspected he was a major part of the problem. In business, he was an expert mediator. When it came to voicing his feelings, most would find him lacking. But whatever happened from this point forward with Corri, he had to make it right, before she left him for good.

* * *

Corri snapped her cell phone closed immediately before the knock came at the door. She called "Come in," heard the click of the code, and sensed that Aidan was about to make a grand appearance. And he did, dressed in an immaculate black suit and the corny red baseball tie she'd given him for Christmas. As wonderful as he looked, she was in no mood to be nice. She wasn't inclined to turn from the mirror or stop removing her stage makeup. Not until she had a solid grip on her temper.

"Good show," he said as he took a couple of steps toward her.

She swiped the cold-cream-coated tissue across her cheeks and forehead. "Thank you. I thought it went well, all things considered."

"Where were you last night?" he asked, although his tone wasn't at all stern.

"Out." She'd gone to a mindless movie alone, all the while thinking about him and resisting the temptation to return his call.

"What's going on, Corri?"

After tossing the tissue aside, she spun on the stool to confront him. "I just received an interesting call from my agent. It seems I have an offer from the cable network. It also seems that he told you about the possibility a few weeks before he left for his holiday vacation. He was surprised you didn't mention it to me, and frankly, so was I."

"I didn't say anything because it wasn't a firm deal."

That did nothing to assuage her anger. "And you didn't think it warranted even a passing comment?"

He shoved his hands into his pockets. "Look, Corri, whatever transpires between you and your agent is your business."

And business, as always, was foremost on his mind. "I have until the second week of January to accept or decline."

"It's a once-in-a-lifetime opportunity, Corri."

"And my contract?"

"Will be dissolved when you accept."

When she accepted. Apparently he was counting on that. "Then you're not going to even counter the deal?"

"I can't match it, Corri."

"You don't even know what it is yet. Or do you?"

"No. But I've been in the business long enough to know what comes with the deal. You'll have your own staff, probably twice as much money as you make now, if not more."

But she wouldn't have him, as if she really ever had. "And a totally different show since it appears they don't want my current format."

"They can't have it because it belongs to me."

"And I'm sure you'll find a replacement in short order if I leave."

"Probably not. It wouldn't work with anyone else."

Now for the nitty-gritty. "And you can't give me any other reason to stay?"

He hesitated for a moment before saying, "I knew when you took on the show that it was only a stepping stone. Only a matter of time before you hit the big time."

Tamara's advice came back to Corri then, as sharp as a knife's blade.

He's grooming you.... And once you reach the pinnacle, he'll bow out of your life and move on to someone else....

She gripped the arms of the stool with the force of her fury, and the realization she'd been a total fool again. "Oh, I get it now. You didn't hesitate to sleep with me because you've known all along it would only be temporary. You knew that I would be out of your life, and you wouldn't have to deal with the possible repercussions at the office or with your family." She pulled the diamond and ruby necklace from beneath her blouse. "And I suppose this is some kind of consolation prize, a little token of your esteem that might ease the blow when I realized I've been screwed, both literally and figuratively."

Aidan's expression turned stony, his jaw tight. "Is that what you really think?"

"What am I supposed to think, Aidan, when you're not saying anything to the contrary?"

"I'm sorry you feel that way," he said, then turned to the door and clasped the knob. "Let me know when you've finalized the deal."

He left without further comment. Without even telling her that she'd meant more to him than a fling. Unlike Kevin, he'd ended it in person, but it didn't hurt any less. In fact, it hurt ten times more—because she hadn't been in love with Kevin.

Nine

Corri found nothing happy about the impending new year, but at least she had plans for the evening, even if she didn't exactly embrace the thought of the charity auction. Or what she was about to do.

Setting the box on the vanity, she opened the dressing-room drawer where she'd stored a few mementos from the past year. She came upon the lucky penny she'd found in the parking lot the day she'd auditioned and dropped it into the box. Obviously her luck had run out, at least when it came to her personal life. She pulled out the newspaper article announcing the debut of the show, complete with a picture of her standing between Aidan and Freed. Had she known then what she knew now—that she would be caught up in an unrequited love for the studio's owner—she wondered if she would take it all back. No, not all of it. If she had a chance for a do-over, she would categorically erase her history with Kevin. But not with Aidan, even if her heart was breaking one fissure at a time.

Since the last taping, she'd only seen Aidan in passing, and during those times they'd exchanged polite greetings that amounted to little more than a few "how are yous." Even before their relationship had turned from friendship to intimacy, they had always stopped long enough to talk. Now they were virtually strangers.

"I can't believe you're working on a holiday, Corri."

At the sound of the familiar voice, she looked up to see Mallory standing in the door Corri had left open. She'd hoped that Aidan might see the open door as an invitation and at least give her a proper goodbye, even if he couldn't give her anything else.

Corri forced a smile around the sudden ache in her heart. "What brings you to the studio on New Year's Eve?"

"Whit's meeting with a man who's going to refurbish the waiting area. Aidan asked him to oversee it." She stepped inside and zeroed in on the box. "Did you make a resolution to do some New Year's clean-up?"

Corri never made resolutions because she didn't believe in them. But she did resolve to move on with her life. "Actually, I'm moving to California in a few weeks. I've decided to get a head start on packing."

Mallory looked flabbergasted. "What in heaven's name is in California?"

"My new job, as soon as I officially accept it." Something she still hadn't done, although she saw no reason to wait past the first of the week. "I'm going to be working for a cable network."

"What does Aidan have to say about this?"

"Nothing." And that was the problem.

"He hasn't tried to convince you to stay?"

Corri lifted one shoulder in a shrug. "He realizes it's a good opportunity for me, and the studio can't match the offer."

Mallory leaned back against the vanity. "What about your relationship? Are you willing to leave that behind, too?"

"I don't have a choice, Mallory. What Aidan and I shared is over. I've known from the beginning it was only temporary." And that knowledge didn't make the ending any less painful.

"But you're still in love with him," Mallory said.

Corri rummaged through the keepsakes to avoid Mallory's assessment. "How I feel doesn't matter, because he doesn't feel the same way."

"Have you asked him?"

Corri's gaze zipped from the drawer to Mallory. "I shouldn't have to ask him anything. If he cares about me, then it's up to him to tell me. I'm not going to bully him into confessing." She didn't want to hear him say that all she'd meant to him was a few frantic tumbles between the sheets.

When Mallory spun around and headed to the door, Corri asked, "Where are you going?"

She turned and smiled. "I grew up with five brothers, Corri. I know all about bullies, and believe me, I have no problem playing that role."

Before Corri could issue a protest or tell Mallory that her attempts to persuade Aidan would be futile, she'd disappeared. She picked up the box and decided to leave in order to prepare for the evening—before the fireworks began in the office down the hall.

"I'd never dreamed such extreme stupidity would plague so many male members of our family."

Aidan looked up from his laptop to find his sister standing in his office doorway, scowling. "I'm not the only man in the city who works on New Year's Eve, Mallory."

She stormed into the office, pulled back the chair opposite him, and lowered herself into it. "That's not what I'm referring to."

He had a feeling she wasn't there to pay him a social call. "Where's your husband?"

"Talking to the contractor, per your instructions. I've decided to take a few moments and talk to you about Corri. She just told me that she's moving to California in a couple of weeks."

Corri had apparently come to the decision to take the job without telling him. Not that he'd expected anything less. They hadn't spoken to any degree since their confrontation four days ago in the dressing room. And not a minute had gone by when he hadn't chastised himself for not saying more. For not trying another shot at making amends. "It's a chance of a lifetime, Mallory."

"And you're going to let her go—" she snapped her fingers "—just like that?"

As far as he could see, he didn't have a choice. "It's her decision to make, not mine."

Mallory braced her elbows on the edge of the desk and grabbed her auburn hair at her scalp, as if she wanted to pull it out by the roots, before she slapped her palms on the wooden surface. "For once would you stop thinking like a businessman and start thinking like a man. If you could possibly manage to do that for a change, then you'd realize Corri's in love with you."

He had a hard time dealing with the concept. "She told you that?"

"She didn't have to tell me. It's obvious to everyone, except to you. And you know what else is obvious, Aidan?"

No, but he had a strong feeling she was going to tell him. "What?"

"You're in love with her, too, and it's time for you to face it. You're thirty-five years old, you have money, your own business, a house that's big enough for two families, and you're too scared to settle down with the best woman you've ever had in your life."

He damned the truth in her words. Damned himself for not having the capacity to control the situation. "I have no right to stand in her way, Mallory. It wouldn't be fair for me to even try."

"It wouldn't be fair to either one of you if you don't give her the choice."

"She might not be as successful if she stays with the studio."

Mallory reached over and laid a hand on his arm, although he got the feeling she might like to coldcock him. "You can offer her more than a career. You can offer her a future with you, unless you're going to lie like a dog and claim that you don't have feelings for her." When he let his lack of denial do the talking, she sent him a pleading look. "Tell her, Aidan. Tell her what she needs to hear, and what you really need to say. It's not that difficult when you stand to lose so much."

Aidan acknowledged his sister was right, but he still saw one major problem. "It's hard to have a serious conversation with someone who's not speaking to you."

"You're a smart man, big brother, at least most of the time. I'm sure you'll figure it all out." Mallory rose from the chair as quickly as her pregnant state would allow and headed toward the door but paused before walking away. "Just don't take too long, Aidan. Otherwise, she'll be gone, and you'll be left wondering what might have been."

For the first time in his life, Aidan was faced with making a monumental decision that didn't involve work. But he had a few ideas, and more than a few connections, as well as a prime opportunity tonight to spill his guts. Unfortunately, only four hours remained before the function, and he had the overwhelming feeling that he was definitely running out of options—and time.

Corri stood next to the dais on the gold-bedecked stage—last in line to be auctioned off like a piece of meat dressed in a floor-length, long-sleeved black gown with a high neck and a nice touch of shimmer. But still no less than a piece of meat.

It's a good cause, she'd told herself for the past hour while awaiting her turn on the block. Her obligation entailed serving only as a dinner companion to the highest bidder. And then it hit her. What if she didn't receive a bid? That would be her luck of late. Tomorrow morning, she would open up the society page and beneath the New Year's tidings, she'd find an article covering the event, with priority given to the poor hapless chef who couldn't even garner a date for charity.

"Ladies and gentleman, our next generous volunteer is the host of the infamous show, *Hot Cooking with Corri*. I give you Corinna Harris."

Corri wasn't particularly fond of the term *infamous,* or the spotlight that blinded her, but at least she'd received a nice round of applause.

"We'll open the bid with five hundred dollars." The auctioneer gestured with his gavel. "I have five hundred, do I hear six?"

Corri began to relax with the knowledge that at least someone found her worthy of a few hundred bucks, even if she couldn't see who that someone was. But when the bidding took on a frenzied pace, climbing higher and higher, she began to feel edgy and anxious. And her strong case of nerves only escalated when some unknown party shouted, "Ten thousand dollars."

The crowd grew deathly silent, and Corri had to remember to close her gaping mouth. "Ten thousand going once, going twice…" The host rapped his gavel, startling Corri almost out of her stiletto heels. "Sold to the gentleman in the corner."

Corri had no idea who the anonymous donor might be, until another well-dressed man walked onto the stage, whispered something in the auctioneer's ear, who in turn replied, "Congratulations to our final bidder who has set a record with his generosity. Please give a hand to Mr. J. D. Breckenridge, the Third."

Corri's eyes widened despite her efforts to look calm. She knew J. D. Breckenridge by reputation, and had met him once at a cocktail party she'd attended with Kevin. He was reputedly a playboy extraordinaire, with an obscene amount of money inherited from a family who owned half of Houston's real estate.

When the house lights came up over the hotel ballroom and her vision adjusted, Corri walked down the steps leading to the main floor. Once there, she was greeted by a hulking bald man with football-field shoulders. "Ms. Harris, I've been sent to deliver a message from Mr. Breckenridge. He's waiting for you in the lobby."

"Thank you," she muttered. "I'll be there in a few minutes." Right after she retrieved a glass of wine to calm her jitters.

After working her way through the crowd, she spotted a roving waiter who happened to be carrying a tray filled with champagne. She snatched a flute on the fly and then located a bench where she sat and checked her makeup. Even if she wasn't all that enthused over this date, she still wanted to look presentable. For all she knew, she might even like the guy. Not a chance. Her thoughts were still centered on Aidan, even though her wounds were still raw and probably would be for months to come, if not years.

As she sipped the champagne, she wondered where he was tonight. If he'd already replaced her by now. If he would be seeing in the new year with another woman at his house. More specifically, in his hot tub.

Thrusting the thoughts away, she set the now-empty flute aside, came to her feet and headed for the lobby. She vowed to forget about Aidan tonight and try to enjoy herself, at least for a while.

Although the lobby was brimming with people, Corri had no trouble spotting Mr. Breckenridge. He had an eternal tan and his hair was a near match to hers, although she suspected he was a bottle-blond-highlights kind of guy. She could definitely do worse. The poor news anchor who'd been auctioned off before her had been bought by an eighty-year-old multimillionaire known for marrying and divorcing young trophy wives at an alarming rate. At least she could rest assured that her date wouldn't be oxygen-dependent.

When he caught her glance, J.D. presented a winning smile that most surely had wooed many a woman. As far as Corri was concerned, his teeth were a tad too perfect. Probably enhanced by expensive veneers. She certainly didn't plan to inspect them tonight, even if he'd paid two hundred thousand dollars for her company instead of ten thousand.

As she approached him, she realized that with her heels and his height, she might be an inch or so taller. Regardless, she would be keeping her shoes and all articles of clothing in place tonight.

"It's nice to see you again, Ms. Harris." He immediately took her hand and gave it a kiss.

She found nothing charming about the gesture, although she suspected he did. "Then you remember that we've met before."

"I've never forgotten it, or you. But I recall you were engaged to some writer. Kyle, I believe it was?"

She tugged her hand from his. "Kevin, and we're no longer engaged." Although when J.D. sent her a steamy look, she questioned the wisdom in making that revelation.

"Are you ready to commence with our date?" he asked.

As ready as she would ever be. "Of course."

He laid his palm on the small of her back and when he started toward the revolving doors leading to the street, she pulled up short. "The banquet room's in the other direction."

He raised an unnaturally thin brow. "Now do you really want to eat a mass-produced meal, or would you prefer a French dinner in an intimate setting?"

Normally she would opt for the latter, but something about this man didn't ring quite true. "Your point is well taken, but the dinner is included with your donation."

"I can afford to miss a free meal."

But could she afford to leave the premises with him? "Where exactly is this restaurant?"

"It's a surprise, but I promise you'll enjoy it."

"But is it nearby?" Within running distance back to the hotel would be good.

"Not that far." He took her hand again and led her outside beneath the hotel's portico, where a black stretch limo waited at the curb, the big bald linebacker holding open the door.

She wrested from J.D.'s grasp as politely as possible. "At least give me a hint as to where we're going since I really don't know you at all."

Unmistakable frustration turned his expression hard.

"Look, I've paid a good deal of money for your companionship, and that didn't include playing twenty questions."

Now she knew what his initials stood for—Jerk Deluxe. "I think I'm entitled to know where I'm going before I'm whisked away by a stranger."

He had the audacity to wrap one arm around her waist. "Don't worry. I'm not going to harm you. I am going to give you a holiday to remember."

Exactly what Aidan had said on Christmas day, only it didn't sound at all inviting coming from his fake mouth. "Only dinner, Mr. Breckenridge."

"It's J.D., Corri. I think we should be on a first-name basis." He winked. "You know something. We'd make beautiful children together."

Corri clinched her teeth and spoke through them. "Either unhand me now, or I'll make sure you'll never father any children."

He had the gall to laugh. "I like you, Corri. You have a lot of spirit."

Just when Corri was considering a knee-plant to his groin, she heard the sound of rapid footsteps coming from behind her, followed by, "Get your hands off her, you sorry son of a bitch."

Ten

When Breckenridge dropped his arm from around Corri, Aidan stepped between them, his fists balled at his sides, itching to throw a punch. "The lady's not going anywhere with you."

Breckenridge looked too smug for a man who was a good five inches shorter, but then he also had a body-guard on alert nearby. "If you'd been on time for the auction, O'Brien, you might be in my place."

Corri stared at him in disbelief. "You were there?"

"I came in after the fact, otherwise I would have topped this bastard's bid."

Breckenridge looked a lot less confident that before. "But you weren't on time, proving once again that the man who comes in late finishes last."

Aidan turned to Corri. "Am I too late?"

She kept her gaze leveled on his. "That depends on what you have in mind."

"I have a few things I need to say to you, but not here."

"Then where?"

"Back in the hotel."

"Wait a minute," Breckenridge said. "You can't leave with him when I've already paid for you."

Aidan took out his checkbook and a pen from the tux's inside pocket, walked to limo and used the hood to write. He tore out the check and offered it to J.D. "Here's your reimbursement, plus another five grand for your trouble. If you go back inside, I'm sure you'll find someone who'll have dinner with you for free." Until that someone wised up and realized the jackass had an over-inflated opinion of himself.

Aidan took Corri's hand into his. "Let's go."

She didn't issue a protest, only allowed him to guide her back into the hotel. But when they reached the elevator, she sent him a questioning look. "Where are we going?"

"Upstairs." To the top floor, where he'd rented the best suite in preparation to speak from the heart, not from his head for a change.

After they boarded the elevator, Corri leaned against one wall, keeping a wide berth between them. "I can't believe you just wrote out a check for fifteen thousand dollars."

He took a chance and ran his fingertip along her jaw. "Believe me, Corri, you're worth it."

And she was, even if this happened to be their last few minutes together.

* * *

She wasn't at all astonished that he looked so wonderful in his black silk tuxedo. She wasn't stunned that he'd rented the penthouse suite. She wasn't shocked that he'd come to her rescue again, as he had so many times before when she'd had a bad day at work, or an argument with Kevin. Yet she sensed that the night could be filled with more surprises, although she wasn't ready to give in to the hope trying to break down the barriers around her heart.

"Have a seat," Aidan said, indicating the gold brocade sofa in the center of the room.

Corri set her bag on the wet bar and crossed the lengthy room. Once she was seated, she expected Aidan to join her. Instead, he paced a while before taking the chair across from her.

After loosening his tie, he leaned forward and scrubbed both hands over his face before settling back against the cushion. "I've got a lot of things to say to you, Corri, and you're going to have to be patient because frankly, I suck at this."

"Take as long as you need, Aidan." Unless he'd brought her here to apologize and give her a fond farewell, maybe even offer a last round of hot sex for the road. If that happened to be the case, she wanted out of there as fast as her heels would let her, before the threatening tears began to fall in earnest.

"First of all, I don't want you to leave the studio," he began. "I'll do whatever I can to change your mind."

She should have known this was all about business. "You're the one who decided not to counter the offer."

"Let me rephrase that. I don't want you to leave *me*."

Okay, so maybe she wasn't going to run after all or cry. At least not yet. "Tell me why you don't want me to leave, Aidan."

"Because for the past year, I've looked forward to seeing you almost every day, even when you were with Kevin. And I'm not sure how well I'll handle not seeing you again."

She could tell these admissions were costing him simply by the way he kept tugging at his collar. "I can always visit."

"I'm not only talking about work, Corri. I'm talking about having you in my life for good. I'm sick of pretending I don't have feelings for you because I do. I'm tired of pretending, period."

She felt as if she'd been dropped into some surreal dimension, where the strong, stoic Aidan had been replaced by a man wearing his heart on his tailored sleeve and in his green eyes. "I'm tired of pretending, too, Aidan, and—"

He held up a hand to halt her words. "Let me get this out while I can." After pushing off the chair, he rounded the coffee table, sat beside her and took her hand. "If you want to go to California, I'd be willing to relocate the studio and go with you."

As predicted, some alien had kidnapped Aidan. "Why would you do that?"

"Because I don't want to watch you walk away."

She couldn't take a step now, even if her life depended it on it. She also couldn't prevent the lump forming in her throat, preventing her from speaking.

He looked away for a moment before centering his eyes back on hers. "I don't want to be only your friend, Corri. I can't be when I'm in love with you."

She cleared her tightening throat. Now if only she could as easily clear away the fog in her brain. "Could you repeat that?"

This time, his gaze didn't waver. "I love you. I have since the day you walked into the studio and auditioned for the show. It took me a while to realize that, but I'm ready to admit it now."

She felt giddy, lightheaded, weepy and amazingly decisive. "I don't want to go to California. I don't want to leave you, either. And for the record, I fell in love with you the day you left the first bag of my favorite caramel candy in the dressing room."

He looked almost offended. "Not when I kissed you that first time in the kitchen?"

"Actually, that's when I fell in lust with you."

He released a deep, sexy laugh that made Corri's insides flutter. "You're still in lust with me."

She'd forgive him his cockiness. Heck, she'd forgive him just about anything right now. "And I could say the same thing to you. And you know something? I think that passion and friendship can go hand-in-hand."

"I know they can." He sighed. "And that's what went wrong with Tamara and me. We weren't friends. Not like you and I are. And that's not ever going to end, Corri."

"No, it's not," she said with all the certainty she felt at that moment.

He tugged her against his side. "And neither is the chemistry. Not if I have any say in the matter, which I do."

He topped off the declaration with a very passionate kiss, and this time Corri welcomed the fire. But right when things began to get interesting, Aidan broke the kiss and pulled her to her feet. "I have something to give you in the bedroom."

"I was hoping you'd say that."

He smiled as he guided her into the adjacent room where she discovered that the king-size bed contained a layer of gold wrapped caramel candies, which she found much more appropriate than roses. "I can't believe you did this."

"I'm not done yet."

Corri turned her attention to Aidan who withdrew a black velvet box and held it in the well of his palm. "If I give you this, you have to promise me you're not going to throw it across the room."

She pulled the necklace he'd given her from beneath the bodice of her high-collared dress. "I still have this." Although she had considered mailing it back to him from California.

He opened the hinged lid to reveal a large marquis diamond ring, surrounded by tiny rubies, centered in the box. Corri could only stare at it, still reluctant to believe that this particular piece of jewelry meant what she thought it might, until he said, "Marry me, Corri, and I'll do everything in my power to make you happy."

"You already do, Aidan."

Without the least bit of hesitation, she took the ring and slid it onto her finger, knowing that this time it belonged there, where Kevin's had not. She and Aidan belonged together.

Aidan tossed the box onto the bed, then kissed her again with a tenderness that sealed the feelings that should have been acknowledged months ago, before they'd wasted so much time. Then again, maybe the timing simply hadn't been right.

It was now.

She pulled back and smiled. "Are we going to have to eat all that candy before we can use the bed?"

"That would take too long."

She tugged his tie away and loosened the collar's top button. "You're right. Maybe we should find someone to share it with."

He turned her around and lowered the zipper on her dress. "We can take it with us to my parents' tomorrow for the New Year's Day celebration."

Corri's dress dropped to the ground, along with her spirits. She faced Aidan with a frown. "I guess we'll have to play the only-friends game for a little while longer."

"Not this time, babe. I'm going to tell my family everything. I'm not going to hide my feelings anymore."

He didn't have to—she could see them in his eyes. "I love you, Aidan. More than my favorite paring knife."

"And I love you enough to put up with your habit of leaving your shoes lying around. But promise me you'll keep the knife away from innocent vegetables. And me."

"I promise. Now promise you're going to take off your clothes and take me to bed, O'Brien."

"You don't have to ask me twice."

And she didn't. With a few sweeps of his arm, he raked the candy onto the floor, scattering it like gold hailstones over the carpet. With a few fast moves, he had them both undressed and down on the bed without even bothering to turn back the covers. And with some very creative touches and kisses, he had Corri practically begging him to cease the sensual torment.

If anyone had told her a few months ago that she would be making love for the second time in a week, in an extravagant hotel suite with Aidan O'Brien, completely in love and committed to marriage, she would have ordered them a psychiatric evaluation. But that's exactly where she was, and she couldn't imagine wanting to be anywhere else on earth.

Corri wasn't certain she wanted to be in the O'Brien's living room, even though Aidan's parents, along with Mallory and Whit, were the only family members in attendance. When Aidan delivered his oration in a commanding tone that left no room for debate about their marriage plans, she eyed the exit. No one said a word in response. Mallory simply stood there, eyes wide, with Whit's arms wrapped around her, as if he might need to keep her upright.

Lucy exchanged a knowing look with Dermot before she moved off the sofa and shook her head. "This won't do, Aidan."

If a little gentle persuasion didn't work, Corri would be out the door before Lucy suffered a breakdown—and she had one of her own. "I know it seems very sudden, Lucy," she said. "But we're counting on your blessing."

"I'm not unhappy about the marriage, Corri. I'm unhappy about the location of the wedding. I will not have my son and future daughter-in-law marrying in a chapel in Las Vegas."

Corri let out the breath she'd been holding and took Aidan's hand for support.

"I've reserved half of a hotel, Mother, not a chapel," he said. "And we've both decided that with our schedules, having it at the same time as the conference in April makes sense."

Lucy looked none too pleased. "Why do you feel the need to attend this conference?"

He gave Corri's hand a squeeze. "Because that's where I need to be in order to sell Corri's show. If I play my cards right, it could mean nationwide syndication."

That thought did nothing to quiet Corri's floundering composure. "The conference will only last three days, and after that, we'll have the wedding. Then Aidan and I will be leaving on our honeymoon." Those plans had yet to be nailed down, not that Corri cared. As long as the arrangements included a whirlpool, and Aidan, she'd be pleased as punch.

"I'm going to fly everyone out at my expense," Aidan continued. "Even Kevin, although I doubt he'll come."

This was one time Corri hoped he didn't show up. That would simply be too weird for words.

"I'll have the babies," Mallory said, the first words she'd spoken. "We'll have to have the nanny hired by then."

Lucy looked appalled. "A nanny will be raising my granddaughters?"

"Only part-time, Lucy," Whit said. "Mallory's afraid I'm not going to be able to handle all that diaper duty."

Mallory patted his cheek. "Your aversion to baby poo does not instill confidence, honey."

Before the conversation digressed into an all-out debate on nannies and dirty diapers, Corri opted to return to the topic at hand. "I'd like for you to be my maid of honor, Mallory." A fitting request considering she'd played a large role in setting her brother straight, according to Aidan.

Mallory left her husband to give Corri a hug. "I'd be honored to be your maid of honor."

"I'd like for you to be the best man, Dad," Aidan said.

Dermot wrapped his arms around his wife and let go a loud laugh. "Of course you would, son. In this family, I am the very best man. Just ask your ma."

Lucy gave him an affectionate poke in the belly. "Hush, old man, and get the champagne."

Per his wife's orders, Dermot left the room and returned with the open champagne bottle and several red plastic glasses left over from Christmas. He poured everyone a drink—aside from Mallory who settled for a glass of water—and lifted his cup for a toast.

"I will not be handin' you any clever Irish words today, Corri and Aidan. But I will be telling you that sometimes the path we take leads us in the wrong direction, but now that you're on the right road, remember this. You two have been given a gift that you must cherish each day of your lives together. You must argue now and again to let the other know you care, and you must be makin' up as often to keep your love alive." He turned his attention to Lucy. "And son, you must treat our Corri well, for we will not take kindly to losing her a second time."

Aidan wrapped his arm around Corri and kissed her gently. "It's taken me too long to find her to lose her again."

"And one more thing," Dermot said. "When you're not producing those shows, then I expect you to be producing me another grandchild."

Aidan winked at Corri. "We'll keep that in mind. But you're going to have to wait a year or two."

Corri couldn't agree more. She would like nothing better than to have a baby, but she wasn't ready to share her soon-to-be husband for a while.

When Dermot raised his glass, everyone followed suit. "To an April wedding in Vegas."

Corri stood immediately outside the five-star hotel's private dining room, which had been transformed into the perfect place for a perfect wedding. She wore a custom-made dress that some might view as risqué with its strapless red and white paisley bodice and slim floor-length silk skirt and the ruby and diamond necklace circling her throat. But Aidan had always said she looked good in red, and she wasn't going to disappoint him. When he took his place at the front of the room, Dermot at his side, he definitely didn't disappoint her. He'd chosen a steel-gray tux and matching tie, with a single rose pinned to his lapel. He'd grown his hair a little longer, and that was fine by her. More to run her hands through later.

"Are you ready, Corinna?"

"I'm ready." She placed her hand in the bend of her father's arm, still amazed that he'd come, even knowing her mother had also agreed to attend. Bridgette and James

Harris in the same room could be a recipe for disaster. Fortunately, they'd been cordial to each other, and no blood had been shed in the making of this wedding.

Mallory—who wore a form-fitting red silk gown that demonstrated how quickly she'd recovered from the birth of the twins, Lucy and Madison—gave Corri an embrace. "Remember to breathe," she murmured, and then started down the rose-bedecked aisle to the strains of soft classical music, complements of the string quartet Aidan had hired.

When her father urged her forward, Corri measured her steps to Aidan. She passed by the rows of white chairs containing most of the O'Brien family, with the exception of Kevin. A few of Aidan's present and former colleagues were also in attendance, but thankfully not Tamara. The past was just that—in the past—and only the future awaited Corri, a future that seemed as bright as the candles lining the front of the room.

Once they reached the wedding party, James kissed Corri's cheek and after she gave her bouquet to Mallory, he placed her hand in Aidan's. Keeping their gazes focused on each other, they exchanged traditional vows, and rings—Aidan's a plain gold band, Corri's a circle of diamonds and of course, rubies. But when Corri geared up for the best part—the requisite kiss—the justice of the peace said, "Aidan would like to take a moment to say a few more words to you, Corri."

She glanced at Mallory, who looked as astonished as Corri felt. But when Aidan squeezed her hand, she gave him her full attention.

He cleared his throat, but his gaze never left hers.

"There have been only a few times in my life that I've been honestly surprised, Corri. But you've surprised me since the day that I met you. I wasn't expecting that I would be standing here with you now, but I'm glad I am." He paused and touched her face with reverence. "I realize I'm not good at expressing my feelings, and that's why I want everyone to know that I love you, and I always will. That's all I have to say."

As far as Corri was concerned, that said it all.

She was mildly aware of the sounds of sniffles coming from Mallory, but very aware that her own tears had begun to fall. "I love you, too, Aidan." And she did, more than she could express.

Without waiting for any prompting, Aidan kissed her to a round of applause, and Dermot shouting, "Let's get on with the celebratin'." As they headed back down the aisle, Lucy blew her a kiss, her mother and father smiled, and Logan, along with Kieran, gave them both a thumbs-up.

When they reached the vestibule, Aidan took Corri into a secluded alcove near the elevator and kissed her again, this time with enough heat to melt the nearby Grecian urn.

"You could have warned me you were going to say all those wonderful things," Corri said when they parted. "I only repeated what I was told."

"I wanted to say it. And I have something else to tell you, too."

Corri wasn't certain she could handle another shock to her system. "Is it good news?"

"You could say that. I've got five bi-coastal deals in

the works for the show. That means you're going to be a household name, if I have anything to say about it."

Corri loved every word that came out of his gorgeous mouth. "I can't believe it."

"Believe it." He ran his palm over her bottom before bringing it to her lower back. "What do you have on under this dress?"

A red garter, and not much else. "As soon as we're through with the reception, you can take me upstairs and see for yourself."

He went into full-out sensual assault on her neck. "Are you sure we're required to attend?"

She wasn't sure about anything at the moment, other than that people were beginning to stare. "Yes, we have to attend. We can't miss your father's toast."

He lifted his head and smiled. "Fine, as long as we have a few hours alone before our flight leaves tonight."

The flight was the means to arrive at an unknown destination, a location Corri had not been able to wring out of Aidan, no matter what tack she had taken, and she'd taken several. "You're still not going to tell me where we're going, are you?"

"No. It's another surprise."

For someone who hadn't always welcomed surprises, Corri looked forward to this one—as well as a lifetime full with Aidan.

Epilogue

Aidan reached the control room in the nick of time to watch his wife in action. And as always, she didn't disappoint her fans. She hadn't disappointed him, either. So far, marriage had definitely agreed with them both, and it showed in Corri's smile when she caught his glance as she walked to the front of the set to take questions.

He immediately noticed her wringing her hands when she said, "Ladies and gentlemen, we're going to do something a little different today in the time we have left."

"Where have we heard that before," the sound engineer muttered.

After Corri turned to the refrigerator, Parker let go a loud groan. "You've only been married to her two months, Aidan. What did you do?"

Nothing bad that he could immediately recall. He'd

given her an elaborate wedding, taken her on a fourteen-day Mediterranean cruise for the honeymoon and had told her he loved her every day. The only thing remotely resembling an argument between them had come when he'd almost tripped over her shoes. Other than that, he didn't have a clue.

Again she returned with an armload of vegetables, and the sudden sense of déjà vu had Aidan poised to halt the taping, even if he didn't believe she'd repeat the same mistake she'd made in December. "Give her a minute, Parker. Corri's a professional."

"That's what you said the last time," he muttered.

Corri lined the tomatoes, lettuce and cucumber in a neat row. "I want to talk about fresh vegetables now that summer is almost upon us." She leveled her gaze on Aidan. "For all you women out there, it's important to include them in your diet, particularly if things have gotten too hot in the kitchen and you discover you've got that proverbial bun in your oven."

Aidan suddenly realized what he had done, but it had nothing to do with the kitchen, although it had been hot. A moonlit balcony, an ocean view, a little too much wine, and a forgotten condom equaled a mistake of the first order. But this was one mistake he didn't care to take back, if in fact he was reading Corri right.

"All that said," Corri continued. "For the next thirty weeks or so, we'll be devoting one show a month to meals for expectant mothers."

Aidan was already out the door and down the stairs leading to the gallery when Corri added, "And now I'd like you to meet the brains behind the newest production, my husband and owner of AOB studios, Aidan O'Brien."

He didn't hesitate to make his way to her. Didn't care that he'd left the crew completely stunned. Didn't give a damn that every member of Corri's viewing public witnessed the less-than-innocent kiss he gave her when he reached the stage.

As cheers rose from the studio audience, Aidan ended the kiss but kept his arms around her. "You're pregnant."

"I am."

With that confirmation came an important question Aidan needed to ask. "Why didn't you tell me sooner?"

"The first few weeks, I was suspicious but not quite ready to accept it. Then I took two pregnancy tests, but I wanted to hear it from a doctor, and I couldn't get an appointment until yesterday. I planned to tell you last night, but you were home so late, and you had two early meetings." She gave him a slight smile. "You're not angry, are you?"

"Not angry. Only concerned."

She patted his cheek. "I'm fine, and quite healthy. Maybe the public announcement's a bit unorthodox, but it can't hurt my ratings."

"If you'd taken the cleaver to the cucumber for my screw-up on the cruise, then that might have hurt your ratings."

She grinned. "Consider yourself lucky. I thought about wrapping the cucumber in plastic and stressing the importance of protecting it against unforeseen growth."

When the applause died down, Corri turned back to the audience, keeping her arm around his waist. "That's all for today. And remember, if you can't be with the one you love, then love the food you're with." She patted his chest. "But I highly suggest you get one of these, so you can enjoy both."

"That's a wrap," the stage director called over the crowd's laughter.

While the audience began to file out, Corri led Aidan through the back hallway and into her dressing room. Once there, he turned her into his arms and thumbed away an unexpected tear from her cheek, worried that maybe she didn't consider this surprise a good thing. "Are you okay, Corri?"

"I couldn't be more thrilled." She left him long enough to grab a tissue from the vanity to dab her eyes. "I couldn't be more hormonal, either."

"So much for waiting a year or two."

She looked at him with a love that he'd never thought he would see or accept. A love that he'd never wanted to see, until Corri. "You should know by now, Aidan, that we don't always have any control over our timing. But I don't think that's necessarily a bad thing."

Neither did he. "Maybe we should call it a day and go home to celebrate."

She presented a coy look that never failed to persuade him. "You could feed me grapes and paint my toenails."

"Don't press your luck, babe. I've already learned to like baths and those damn caramel candies."

He'd learned a lot more from her—when to say what was on his mind and when to shut up. He'd learned a lot about himself; he could spend hours watching her sleep and never get tired of the view. He could commit to something aside from his work, and he was definitely committed to her.

Aidan O'Brien had always been a man of action and few words. He'd always gotten what he wanted, and he'd never wanted anything more than Corri. And now that he had her, he wasn't going to let her go.

* * * * *

Dear Reader,

Several years ago, I came upon an idea for a story while in the middle of writing another book—not at all an uncommon occurrence in my life. I drew on my experience as a surgeon's spouse and a former employee in the health care field to set the story against a medical backdrop. I developed two major characters, wrote a couple of chapters, but beyond that I wasn't certain where the plot should go. I put that partial manuscript aside and returned to the other work-in-progress—which, as fate would have it, went on to become my first Silhouette Desire. I've sold several more books in the interim, yet I never quite let go of the story that hadn't developed beyond its infancy—a heartfelt story that I hoped to finish someday.

"Someday" arrived when Harlequin introduced Everlasting, a new line featuring compelling love stories that go beyond traditional romance. After ten years, I had finally found what I needed to complete that neverforgotten book—direction. In turn, I discovered a perfect fit for *Fall from Grace,* which has now grown into a complex, emotional journey through the lives of a renowned physician and the only woman he ever loved, and eventually lost. Framed in the present, the story includes a recounting of the past—both good and bad times—as the surgeon is forced to put aside his pride and rely on his former wife when sudden illness strikes and threatens his career. It explores overriding themes of hope, healing and strength in the face of tragedy. Above all, it demonstrates that despite past mistakes, in the presence of true love there comes a time to forgive.

I'm thrilled to be a part of the Everlasting launch in February of 2007 with Fall from Grace, and I invite you to discover what this exciting, innovative new line is all about—that every great love has a story to tell.

Kristi Gold

Experience entertaining women's fiction
for every woman who has wondered
"what's next?" in their lives.
Turn the page for a sneak preview
of a new book from Harlequin NEXT,
WHY IS MURDER ON THE MENU, ANYWAY?
by Stevi Mittman

On sale December 26, wherever books are sold.

Ambience is everything. Imagine eating a foie gras at a luncheonette counter or a side of coleslaw at Le Cirque. It's not a matter of food but one of atmosphere. Remember that when planning your dining room design.

—Tips from *Teddi.com*

"Now that's the kind of man you should be looking for," my mother, the self-appointed keeper of my shelf-life stamp, says. She points with her fork at a man in the corner of the Steak-Out Restaurant, a dive I've just been hired to redecorate. Making this restaurant look four-star will be hard, but not half as hard as getting through lunch without strangling the woman across the table from me. "*He* would make a good husband."

"Oh, you can tell that from across the room?" I ask, wondering how it is she can forget that when we had trouble getting rid of my last husband, she shot him. "Besides being ten minutes away from death if he actually eats all that steak, he's twenty years too old for me and—shallow woman that I am—twenty pounds too heavy. Besides, I am *so* not looking for another husband here. I'm looking to design a new image for this place, looking for some sense of ambience, some feeling, something I can build a proposal on for them."

My mother studies the man in the corner, tilting her head, the better to gauge his age, I suppose. I think she's grimacing, but with all the Botox and Restylane injected into that face, it's hard to tell. She takes another bite of her steak salad, chews slowly so that I don't miss the fact that the steak is a poor cut and tougher than it should be. "You're concentrating on the wrong kind of proposal," she says finally. "Just look at this place, Teddi. It's a dive. There are hardly any other diners. What does *that* tell you about the food?"

"That they cater to a dinner crowd and it's lunchtime," I tell her.

I don't know what I was thinking bringing her here with me. I suppose I thought it would be better than eating alone. There really are days when my common sense goes on vacation. Clearly, this is one of them. I mean, really, did I not resolve less than three weeks ago that I would not let my mother get to me anymore?

What good are New Year's resolutions, anyway?

Mario approaches the man's table and my mother studies him while they converse. Eventually Mario leaves the table with a huff, after which the diner glances up and meets my mother's gaze. I think she's smiling at him. That or she's got indigestion. They size each other up.

I concentrate on making sketches in my notebook and try to ignore the fact that my mother is flirting. At nearly seventy, she's developed an unhealthy interest in members of the opposite sex to whom she isn't married.

According to my father, who has broken the TMI rule and given me Too Much Information, she has no interest in sex with him. Better, I suppose, to be clued in on what they aren't doing in the bedroom than have to hear what they might be doing.

"He's not so old," my mother says, noticing that I have barely touched the Chinese chicken salad she warned me not to get. "He's got about as many years on you as you have on your little cop friend."

She does this to make me crazy. I know it, but it works all the same. "Drew Scoones is not my little 'friend.' He's a detective with whom I—"

"Screwed around," my mother says. I must look shocked, because my mother laughs at me and asks if I think she doesn't know the "lingo."

What I thought she didn't know was that Drew and I actually tangled in the sheets. And, since it's possible she's just fishing, I sidestep the issue and tell her that Drew is just a couple of years younger than me and that

I don't need reminding. I dig into my salad with renewed vigor, determined to show my mother that Chinese chicken salad in a steak place was not the stupid choice it's proving to be.

After a few more minutes of my picking at the wilted leaves on my plate, the man my mother has me nearly engaged to pays his bill and heads past us toward the back of the restaurant. I watch my mother take in his shoes, his suit and the diamond pinkie ring that seems to be cutting off the circulation in his little finger.

"Such nice hands," she says after the man is out of sight. "Manicured." She and I both stare at my hands. I have two popped acrylics that are being held on at weird angles by bandages. My cuticles are ragged and there's marker decorating my right hand from measuring carelessly when I did a drawing for a customer.

Twenty minutes later she's disappointed that he managed to leave the restaurant without our noticing. He will join the list of the ones I let get away. I will hear about him twenty years from now when—according to my mother—my children will be grown and I will still be single, living pathetically alone with several dogs and cats.

After my ex, that sounds good to me.

The waitress tells us that our meal has been taken care of by the management and, after thanking Mario, the owner, complimenting him on the wonderful meal and assuring him that once I have redecorated his place people will be flocking here in droves (I actually use those words and ignore my mother when she rolls her eyes), my mother and I head for the restroom.

My father—unfortunately not with us today—has the patience of a saint. He got it over the years of living with my mother. She, perhaps as a result, figures he has the patience for both of them, and feels justified having none. For her, no rules apply, and a little thing like a picture of a man on the door to a public restroom is certainly no barrier to using the john. In all fairness, it does seem silly to stand and wait for the ladies' room if no one is using the men's room.

Still, it's the idea that rules don't apply to her, signs don't apply to her, conventions don't apply to her. She knocks on the door to the men's room. When no one answers she gestures to me to go in ahead. I tell her that I can certainly wait for the ladies' room to be free and she shrugs and goes in herself.

Not a minute later there is a bloodcurdling scream from behind the men's room door.

"Mom!" I yell. "Are you all right?"

Mario comes running over, the waitress on his heels. Two customers head our way while my mother continues to scream.

I try the door, but it is locked. I yell for her to open it and she fumbles with the knob. When she finally manages to unlock and open it, she is white behind her two streaks of blush, but she is on her feet and appears shaken but not stirred.

"What happened?" I ask her. So do Mario and the waitress and the few customers who have migrated to the back of the place.

She points toward the bathroom and I go in, thinking

it serves her right for using the men's room. But I see nothing amiss.

She gestures toward the stall, and, like any self-respecting and suspicious woman, I poke the door open with one finger, expecting the worst.

What I find is worse than the worst.

The husband my mother picked out for me is sitting on the toilet. His pants are puddled around his ankles, his hands are hanging at his sides. Pinned to his chest is some sort of Health Department certificate.

Oh, and there is a large, round, bloodless bullet hole between his eyes.

Four Nassau County police officers are securing the area, waiting for the detectives and crime scene personnel to show up. They are trying, though not very hard, to comfort my mother, who in another era would be considered to be suffering from the vapors. Less tactful in the twenty-first century, I'd say she was losing it. That is, if I didn't know her better, know she was milking it for everything it was worth.

My mother loves attention. As it begins to flag, she swoons and claims to feel faint. Despite four No Smoking signs, my mother insists it's all right for her to light up because, after all, she's in shock. Not to mention that signs, as we know, don't apply to her.

When asked not to smoke, she collapses mournfully in a chair and lets her head loll to the side, all without mussing her hair.

Eventually, the detectives show up to find the four

patrolmen all circled around her, debating whether to administer CPR, smelling salts or simply call the paramedics. I, however, know just what will snap her to attention.

"Detective Scoones," I say loudly. My mother parts the sea of cops.

"We have to stop meeting like this," he says lightly to me, but I can feel him checking me over with his eyes, making sure I'm all right while pretending not to care.

"What have you got in those pants?" my mother asks him, coming to her feet and staring at his crotch accusingly. "*Baydar?* Everywhere we Bayers are, you turn up. You don't expect me to buy that this is a coincidence, I hope."

Drew tells my mother that it's nice to see her, too, and asks if it's his fault that her daughter seems to attract disasters.

Charming to be made to feel like the bearer of a plague.

He asks how I am.

"Just peachy," I tell him. "I seem to be making a habit of finding dead bodies, my mother is driving me crazy and the catering hall I booked two freakin' years ago for Dana's bat mitzvah has just been shut down by the Board of Health!"

"Glad to see your luck's finally changing," he says, giving me a quick squeeze around the shoulders before turning his attention to the patrolmen, asking what they've got, whether they've taken any statements, moved anything, all the sort of stuff you see on TV, without any of the drama. That is, if you don't count my mother's threats to faint every few minutes when she senses no one's paying attention to her.

Mario tells his waitstaff to bring everyone espresso, which I decline because I'm wired enough. Drew pulls him aside and a minute later I'm handed a cup of coffee that smells divinely of Kahlúa.

The man knows me well. Too well.

His partner, whom I've met once or twice, says he'll interview the kitchen staff. Drew asks Mario if he minds if he takes statements from the patrons first and gets to him and the waitstaff afterward.

"No, no," Mario tells him. "Do the patrons first." Drew raises his eyebrow at me like he wants to know if I get the double entendre. I try to look bored.

"What is it with you and murder victims?" he asks me when we sit down at a table in the corner.

I search them out so that I can see you again, I almost say, but I'm afraid it will sound desperate instead of sarcastic.

My mother, lighting up and daring him with a look to tell her not to, reminds him that *she* was the one to find the body.

Drew asks what happened *this time*. My mother tells him how the man in the john was "taken" with me, couldn't take his eyes off me and blatantly flirted with both of us. To his credit, Drew doesn't laugh, but his smirk is undeniable to the trained eye. And I've had my eye trained on him for nearly a year now.

"While he was noticing you," he asks me, "did *you* notice anything about him? Was he waiting for anyone? Watching for anything?"

I tell him that he didn't appear to be waiting or

watching. That he made no phone calls, was fairly intent on eating and did, indeed, flirt with my mother. This last bit Drew takes with a grain of salt, which was the way it was intended.

"And he had a short conversation with Mario," I tell him. "I think he might have been unhappy with the food, though he didn't send it back."

Drew asks what makes me think he was dissatisfied, and I tell him that the discussion seemed acrimonious and that Mario looked distressed when he left the table. Drew makes a note and says he'll look into it and asks about anyone else in the restaurant. Did I see anyone who didn't seem to belong, anyone who was watching the victim, anyone looking suspicious?

"Besides my mother?" I ask him, and Mom huffs and blows her cigarette smoke in my direction.

I tell him that there were several deliveries, the kitchen staff going in and out the back door to grab a smoke. He stops me and asks what I was doing checking out the back door of the restaurant.

Proudly—because, while he was off forgetting me, dropping by only once in a while to say hi to Jesse, my son, or drop something by for one of my daughters that he thought they might like, I was getting on with my life—I tell him that I'm decorating the place.

He looks genuinely impressed. "Commercial customers? That's great," he says. Okay, that's what he *ought* to say. What he actually says is "Whatever pays the bills."

"Howard Rosen, the famous restaurant critic, got her the job," my mother says. "You met him—the good-looking, distinguished gentleman with the *real* job, something to be proud of. I guess you've never read his reviews in *Newsday*."

Drew, without missing a beat, tells her that Howard's reviews are on the top of his list, as soon as he learns how to read.

"I only meant—" my mother starts, but both of us assure her that we know just what she meant.

"So," Drew says. "Deliveries?"

I tell him that Mario would know better than I, but that I saw vegetables come in, maybe fish and linens.

"This is the second restaurant job Howard's got her," my mother tells Drew.

"At least she's getting *something* out of the relationship," he says.

"If he were here," my mother says, ignoring the insinuation, "he'd be comforting her instead of interrogating her. He'd be making sure we're both all right after such an ordeal."

"I'm sure he would," Drew agrees, then looks me in the eyes as if he's measuring my tolerance for shock. Quietly he adds, "But then maybe he doesn't know just what strong stuff your daughter's made of."

It's the closest thing to a tender moment I can expect from Drew Scoones. My mother breaks the spell. "She gets that from me," she says.

Both Drew and I take a minute, probably to pray that's all I inherited from her.

"I'm just trying to save you some time and effort," my mother tells him. "My money's on Howard."

Drew withers her with a look and mutters something

that sounds suspiciously like "fool's gold." Then he excuses himself to go back to work.

I catch his sleeve and ask if it's all right for us to leave. He says sure, he knows where we live. I say goodbye to Mario. I assure him that I will have some sketches for him in a few days, all the while hoping that this murder doesn't cancel his redecorating plans. I need the money desperately, the alternative being borrowing from my parents and being strangled by the strings.

My mother is strangely quiet all the way to her house. She doesn't tell me what a loser Drew Scoones is—despite his good looks—and how I was obviously drooling over him. She doesn't ask me where Howard is taking me tonight or warn me not to tell my father about what happened because he will worry about us both and no doubt insist we see our respective psychiatrists.

She fidgets nervously, opening and closing her purse over and over again.

"You okay?" I ask her. After all, she's just found a dead man on the toilet and tough as she is that's got to be upsetting.

When she doesn't answer me I pull over to the side of the road.

"Mom?" She refuses to meet my eyes. "You want me to take you to see Dr. Cohen?"

She looks out the window as if she's just realized we're on Broadway in Woodmere. "Aren't we near Marvin's Jewelers?" she asks, pulling something out of her purse.

"What have you got, Mother?" I ask, prying open her fingers to find the murdered man's ring.

"It was on the sink," she says in answer to my dropped

jaw. "I was going to get his name and address and have you return it to him so that he could ask you out. I thought it was a sign that the two of you were meant to be together."

"He's dead, Mom. You understand that, right?" I ask. You never can tell when my mother is fine and when she's in la-la land.

"Well, I didn't know that," she shouts at me. "Not at the time."

I ask why she didn't give it to Drew, realize that she wouldn't give Drew the time in a clock shop and add, "...or one of the other policemen?"

"For heaven's sake," she tells me. "The man is dead, Teddi, and I took his ring. How would that look?"

Before I can tell her it looks just the way it is, she pulls out a cigarette and threatens to light it.

"I mean, really," she says, shaking her head like it's my brains that are loose. "What does he need with it now?"

nocturne™

**WAS HE HER SAVIOR
OR HER NIGHTMARE?**

HAUNTED

LISA CHILDS

Years ago, Ariel and her sisters were separated for
their own protection. Now the man who vowed
revenge on her family has resumed the hunt, and
Ariel must warn her sisters before it's too late.
The closer she comes to finding them, the more
secretive her fiancé becomes. Can she trust the man
she plans to spend eternity with? Or has he been
waiting for the perfect moment to destroy her?

On sale December 2006.

REQUEST YOUR FREE BOOKS!

2 FREE NOVELS PLUS 2 FREE GIFTS!

Passionate, Powerful, Provocative!

Silhouette®

SPECIAL EDITION™

Logan's Legacy Revisited

**THE LOGAN FAMILY IS BACK
WITH SIX NEW STORIES.**

Beginning in January 2007 with

THE COUPLE MOST LIKELY TO

by

LILIAN DARCY

Tragedy drove them apart. Reunited eighteen years later, their attraction was once again undeniable. But had time away changed Jake Logan enough to let him face his fears and commit to the woman he once loved?

In February, expect MORE
from

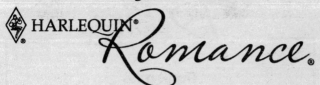

HARLEQUIN® *Romance*®

as it increases to six titles per month.

What's to come...

Rancher and Protector

Part of the

Western Weddings

miniseries

BY JUDY CHRISTENBERRY

The Boss's Pregnancy Proposal

BY RAYE MORGAN

Don't miss February's
incredible line up of authors!

Don't miss
DAKOTA FORTUNES,
**a six-book continuing series following
the Fortune family of South Dakota—
oil is in their blood and privilege
is their birthright.**

This series kicks off with
USA TODAY bestselling author

PEGGY MORELAND'S
Merger of Fortunes
(SD #1771)

this January.